STOLEN WIFE

CARINA BLAKE

Copyrighted © 2020

All Rights Reserved

ISBN: 9798670353274

No part of this book may be reproduced, copied or transmitted in any form or by any means, electronic or mechanical, including photocopying, recording, or by any information storage or retrieval system without written expressed permission from the author, except in the case of brief quotations embodied in critical articles or reviews.

This is a work of fiction. Names, characters, businesses, places, events, and incidents are products of the author's imagination and are used fictitiously. Any resemblance to actual persons, living or dead, events or locales is purely coincidental.

Cover design: Carina Blake

Cover Image: Deposit Photo

The use of actors, artists, movies, TV shows and song titles/lyrics throughout this book are done so for storytelling purposes and should in no way be seen as advertisement. Trademark names are used in an editorial fashion with no intention of infringement of the respective owner's trademark.

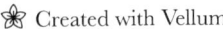 Created with Vellum

Stolen Wife

I'll do whatever it takes to get her in my arms—even kill my brother.

I'll do everything in my power to destroy all who come between us.

The second I held the wedding photo of Giada with my brother, my revenge became tainted with possessiveness so profound that I grew colder. Calculating. Obsessed.

I'll do anything to get my desire. To taste her.

Giada is mine, and it doesn't matter the how or why, because she just is. I'll play her name in my head—my siren's song—as I remove her from my brother's grasp and take her for my own.

One by one, I'll get my revenge on those who sent me away while claiming what was never theirs.

Chapter One

Santino

I GRIP THE FOLDER TIGHTLY IN MY HANDS, BREATHING IN the fresh ink on the papers that my lawyer sent me.

Tomorrow, I'll be a free man.

I've waited two fucking years to get back to my life outside of this cell. Seven hundred and thirty-four days, to be exact, for a murder I didn't commit. I used those two years wisely, though. When I seek out my revenge, every single person who had a hand in my incarceration will pay with their lives.

The son of a bitch who actually confessed to the murder they convicted me of worked for the Avanti crime family. Luckily, he made his dying declaration two weeks ago before finding his way outside of a twenty-story building, taking the quickest way down.

The judge who banged that motherfucking gavel down on my life had to backpedal and let me out based on the new information my lawyer sent him. It's taken a long time due to the bureaucratic red tape to get to this day, and it feels like an eternity.

They knew they never really had a case against me, but they would have done anything to bring down the Marchetti crime family, even if it meant getting to someone in the family. I was convicted on flimsy evidence, planted there by none other than someone in the Marchetti family. What the stupid prosecutors couldn't or wouldn't understand was that I had no interest in helping the family at all. Blood or not, I want nothing to do with those bastards especially after they set me up so easily.

Every dollar I've ever earned has been clean from day one. I worked my whole life to get away from the family business, and now it has swallowed me up and spit me out.

I sit on my thin, worn-out mattress inside my cell to look over the documents. For two years, my team has been out finding evidence to free me and dirt on those who might have put me in here. The packet has more evidence that will get me my company back without a fight and a little something extra to sweeten the deal against any opposition.

According to several of the informants my lawyer wrangled up, my accident at seventeen that forced me off the football team hadn't been an accident at all. My brother had orchestrated the entire thing.

The more I learn about my little brother, the more I know he had something to do with my current situation. Not that I didn't think that from the start. In fact, I knew the evidence had to come from someone on the inside.

When I'd been arrested, it took Rafael two days to visit me with the promise to get me out. I could see through him like a brand-new picture window. The motherfucker has had it out for me since he was able to walk.

As I flip through the file, I come across two sealed

envelopes. I open the first one, and it's my DNA test that they used against me in court with another report attached. Since I was a boy, I've been treated differently, and now I know why. I read the letter attached to the file—I wasn't a Marchetti at all.

I hated to think that my mom could cheat on my father, but he deserved it more than she knew. His resentment toward me finally makes sense. He used to do everything in his power to torment me as a child. I never let it get me down because I always had my mother's love. Her soothing words and soft voice eased the abuse and neglect from my father.

My brother Rafael and I never got along because our father groomed him to hate me. I remember when I was ten years old, we had a pair of vicious Dobermans that were meant to be guard dogs for the family compound. I loved them both and played with them the second I got home from school. One day my father noticed the way they never barked at me and often stood guard over me. He took me out back and then tied my wrists and feet to a chair while giving Rafael a gun to shoot each dog as they growled at them from inside their kennel.

I've wanted dogs for years, but I worked like a madman, traveling around the world too much. I'd just settled down in my new home when the police came with a warrant. I'd love to get a pair now and watch them tear off his flesh. That memory cemented my will to never be like either of them. For the next ten years, I never spoke a word to them unless I was asked a question. I had nothing and wanted nothing more than the basics to survive. My mother, on the other hand, gave me the love I needed to keep me human. Her love for me made me the better man and allowed me to grow up semi-normal.

I can't say that my mother loves him, but she's stayed

all these years. I'm betting that she stayed to protect me. I'm sure if she would have tried to leave him, they would have taken the first opportunity to end my life.

Needing to read all the information in the files, I move on to the next envelope, which is about my brother's illegitimate son, Fabrizio. As I read on, I learn something valuable that I can hang over their heads as I take my time destroying them before they die. I move on through the file and see the report taken by the police from the real killer, and how I'd been set up. There are no names of the conspirators, but the fact that they knew where I was and when made it obvious it was the family.

I reach the end, and one person I don't see anything on is the new Mrs. Marchetti. There's nothing in here about Rafael's wife. They've kept her existence practically non-existent. There's not even a wedding photo. My people haven't even gotten a picture of her coming and going. She didn't have an online presence, and apparently she'd been homeschooled. She's either a total troll or insanely beautiful. Knowing Rafael, she had to be stunning because anything less would be unacceptable. I find it strange that there's not a picture of her anywhere, though. Maybe she's a bigger target than I know, but I doubt it. My guy says it's rumored he won't let her out because he's afraid she'll hoe around on him.

I can't see him letting her fuck around despite the fact he's with his mistress more than he's at home. I've seen his side piece several times over the years before I was locked up. Marie's only twenty-five with a two-year-old and has been mixed up with Rafael since she was seventeen.

I set the documents down with the rest of my things because it's time for my daily exercise. I start with fifty push-ups and then move on to bench-pressing my bed before finishing within an hour with a bit of yoga. I've done everything I can inside my cell when the bell rings.

It's time for lunch, so I'm let out of my cage. Since I've been locked up, I put on thirty pounds full of muscle—most won't even look at me. At first, they believed I was a killer. In the last twenty-four hours, they learned that although I might not have killed anyone, I sent four people to the hospital for fucking with me and mine. You make friends and enemies in this place, even when you keep to yourself.

"Hey, fellas, it's the innocent man in the house!" one of the inmates shouts. They all cheer because respect is respect.

"Thanks. I'm ready to get the fuck out of here," I muttered, walking over to my table. I'm not hungry, but I do snag an apple from the pile. My mind hasn't stopped turning since I got the news. There's so much to do that I'm not sure what needs my attention first.

As I take a bite of my apple, I can feel someone sit next to me. "So, how much did the family pay that guy to take the blame?" Diego, the toughest fucker in this place, says. He's under the impression that I'm a fucking killer at heart. As a part of a mob family, everyone thought I was a murderer no matter who confessed in my place.

"Nothing. I guess the guilt was eating at that motherfucker." I know that he doesn't believe me, but that's not my problem. I take another bite, wondering if he's going to get the point.

"Yeah, so much guilt the fucker took a swan dive off a building. Ha!" He looks around and laughs. Trouble—I can feel it in my bones. "Bullshit. This son of a bitch here got the connects. So do I." His words are laced with bravado. Diego lunges at me, nearly taking me out with a blade. A real knife, but my ass was ready. He only nicks my skin before I slam his head onto the table while my other hand breaks the knife-wielding hand.

"You're a stupid motherfucker," I whisper in his ear through a clenched jaw. "Who paid you?" He doesn't answer, which I expect. Instead, he fights to break the hold even more aggressively, so I break his arm. The guards watch, but don't say shit. I shouldn't even be in this place. "Ready to talk?" I keep my voice down because I'm only concerned about the answer. People do a lot of fucked things to their friends if it gets them a ticket out of here.

"Your brother," he grunts out. I take the knife and stab it into my apple, standing straight up. "You should have that looked at." Kicking his feet out and sending him to hit his head on the bench of the table, I walk away, dropping the apple with the little present into the guard's hand. For everyone to hear, I say, "I'm going to be in my cell because I'm not trying to catch a case in this bitch. Too many cameras."

The hooting and hollering starts as I make my way out of the main eating area. My name is chanted as I make my way back to my little cement box.

I spend the rest of the night in my cell waiting for my release in the morning. I refuse dinner because at this point I don't trust anyone, guards especially. So many motherfuckers are on the take for everything, from just a little nose candy to underage pussy. Some of these guards belong behind bars just like the rest of these guys. I have my lists; I'll have these bastards buried so fast if they try anything.

After a big "fuck you" smile on my face as I pass Diego's cell, I exit the prison in cuffs and two guards. I'm being transported to the courthouse today to be officially freed. My lawyer's ready to file suit for wrongful imprisonment as soon as they bang that gavel.

My friend and personal assistant, Martin Giuseppe, and my lawyer, Dimitri Stanislav, stand at the entrance of the courthouse as I'm escorted out of the prison van. There's a small crowd of reporters looking for a scoop, but I don't have shit to say to them. The officers lead me inside the building and away from the press before they undo the cuffs. After all, the motion is a formality and then I can finally go home.

There's so much to do that I'm anxious to get started. As I make my way inside the courtroom, I notice that my family is nowhere to be seen. They should have come to make themselves look less suspicious in my eyes, but then again, perhaps they don't care, or they expected me to be dead. "Where are my parents?" I ask out of curiosity rather than actual disappointment.

"Your father claims that the families are at war and they'd be a target, or so he said when I called to see if he'd be attending," Dimitri says.

"Yep, I'm betting." We take our seats and wait for our case to be presented. It's insane how I'm not at the front of the line so I can gain my freedom. Every hour I wait, I'm telling Dimitri to add ten grand to the suit. It's not the money. It's the principle.

"The state against Mr. Santino Marchetti." It's my turn, and I'm brought to the front as they quickly read the statements my lawyer and the prosecutor prepared.

The case is over in less than five minutes, making me

annoyed. "What the fuck? I waited hours for that shit. Adding insult to injury." My men lead me out of the courtroom before I lose my fucking mind. There wasn't a single apology, as if I deserved what had happened to me.

My friend that I'd met in prison comes up to us when we enter the hallway. We hug and then I say, "Joey, thanks for showing. Martin, Dimitri, this is my personal guard. He's going to need the clearance like you and Dimitri, if you understand my meaning. Now, who's outside?"

"The D'Angelos and the Avantis," Dimitri says, knowing them all because although he's got nothing to do with the mob, he's been around it his entire life.

"Why? I thought that Rafael's married to the Avanti daughter." That's how I knew my brother was in on it. He's now tied to their family.

"He is, but they don't trust any of the families."

"Is there a contract on my head?" I question, knowing they would have that answer.

"No, but I'm betting they're waiting for your father."

"Or he made a deal with them to off me."

Joey leans in and says, "Everything is prepared." He pulls out two envelopes and hands them to me. I've gathered some interesting info about each family. It's not a lot, but it's enough to warn them that I'm serious.

"Pass the envelopes to both of them when we head out," I tell Martin.

We exit the courthouse with Martin and Dimitri walking in front of me while Joey crowds me. I look right at D'Angelo's man and say, "I'm not a mobster. Leave me alone or I'll show the world what I have learned about your family." I repeat that shit straight to the Avanti family and then look at both families and say, "Excuse me, fuckers. I have a legal business to run."

I say goodbye to Dimitri who came in with Martin, but

Martin will be riding back with me. Joey pulls out and we begin the eight-hour drive with the current traffic back to my home outside NYC. After two minutes we know that we're not being followed, which makes me relax. The ride to my house takes longer as the traffic picks up. The release process took almost five hours, and it's already two. By the time I get home, it's going to be late at night, so I'll have to wait until tomorrow to pay my family a visit.

"I need some food. I haven't eaten much since you gave me the news."

"What do you want to eat?" Joey asks.

"Let's pop into a fast-food burger place. I'm not too picky about it, but I could really use something with fucking flavor."

"Sounds good. We'll do the drive-thru."

"Okay." Five minutes later we pull off on an exit and hit a burger drive-thru, and that shit's no joke. It's been so damn long since I've had a great burger. We eat in the parking lot away from all the other parked vehicles.

"So, I've managed to get my hands on the supplies you needed. They're all at the estate already so we can test them out and go from there," Martin says. He knows where to get high-tech, untraceable devices just in case. I played fair before, but those days are over.

"Sounds good. Now, how about we head back before it gets any later?" Joey nods and then continues the long drive.

It's late by the time we pull through the gates. "Thank you all for what you have done."

Stepping into my house, I release a sigh of pure contentment. "I'll address the staff in the morning. Right now, I just want my bed," I say to Martin. "Please give Joey a room."

"Yes, sir." I walk up to my bedroom and see that everything has been aired out and cleaned. It's wonderful to be in my damn cozy bed. Two years of that shitty mattress almost broke my ass more than anything else.

Chapter Two

Giada

"Be a good girl, and maybe my parents will let you come out of your room for a bit while I'm gone," Rafael says, zipping up his pants after tucking himself inside. Per his commands, I watch him get dressed even though I find him absolutely repulsive.

Not only does he know it, but he truly takes a perverse pleasure in making me uncomfortable. I've grown accustomed to the way he operates, so most days I stare at his shoes. That's the only part of him that's appealing because that means he's leaving.

God, the man is a total patronizing asshole. "When can I call my family?"

He fixes his ugly purple tie that costs more than any piece of clothing I own, and then turns back to me with a raised brow. He's smug and filthy. "Why would you want to do that? To tell them how bad your life is here?"

He turns back to his reflection, smiling through the mirror. I'd love to shatter that thing into a million pieces. I bet he's going to his mistress right after me. I only hate her because she gets freedom. I'm not even concerned about their relationship as long as he doesn't bring an STI to me.

I scoff, knowing full well that my family wouldn't give a damn how I'm treated as long as there's a truce between the families and money to be made. "Why? They wouldn't save me." They willingly sold me to the devil.

"Exactly, so just stop asking." He rolls his suit jacket over his shoulders, giving no fucks about me at all. I feel like punching him in the dick, but I'd probably pay big time. He looks at himself in the mirror, arching his brow and checking his face like he's somehow going to look good. Does he really believe that he's attractive?

"Am I ever going to have a friend?" I'm not sure why I'm pushing it today, but I can't stop myself. Maybe it's the constant solitude. I'd prefer the loneliness if it meant I never had to feel his hands or body on me. There's a lot I'd suffer through to be away from him.

He turns around and walks toward me. Once he's directly in front of me, he sets his knee on the edge of the bed and leans in closely. "You'll have our babies. Once that's done...well...maybe you can make friends with Faustino or Gino." He winks so I understand fully what he means, and I do.

He's struck a nerve like he wanted. My eyes narrow as I lose my temper. "You're such a—" He reaches out and grabs my cheeks with one hand, squeezing my mouth painfully.

"Such a what? I don't know who the hell you think you're talking to. I'm your husband, and you'll learn a little respect or next time I'll make sure you can't sit for a week." He roughly lets go, shoving me backward onto the bed. I rub my jaw, and he laughs as he moves back to the dresser.

"I'll be back in two days for another thorough fucking.

You better be ready for an all-day session. I'm tired of waiting for you to get pregnant. It's good sperm wasted. Now, don't move until it goes off." He reaches over and grabs the egg timer and turns it to fifteen minutes—the length of time I have left before I'm allowed out of bed to clean up after myself.

I toss my head back on the pillow with my legs up in the air and a big pillow under my ass. The sound of the door closes and the lock clicking shut gives way to the pain of my situation.

When Rafael Marchetti is mad, I know that I'll pay with new bruises. At five seven, he's a mean little bastard, using his fists to make up for his other inadequacies.

As a mob boss, he keeps his appearance impeccable to show his control. He doesn't leave until he looks completely put together, even when he's going to visit his dollar-fifty whore. I wish he'd go to his room to do it. We don't share a bedroom, thankfully. If he didn't enjoy his own privacy away from me, he'd sleep in the same bed just to spite me.

As his wife, I take what I'm given and deal with it, or there will be consequences if he doesn't like something I say or do. Some days, I don't put up a fight and that makes him angry, so he is even more violent.

His refusal to let me contact my parents doesn't surprise me. Not that I genuinely want to talk to them, but I need a lifeline somewhere. I'm running out of patience and hope for a change in my situation.

Some days the air in this room is suffocating to the point I'm choking on the pain of the silence. Worse is when I wake up to the nightmares of my wedding night when he beat me after he failed to get off. It took him six tries to break through my hymen with his little cock, and it set him into a rage. I can still remember the pain of his entry over and over.

My family and his made it so I had no other recourse or resource to find a life away from Rafael. My parents run a prostitution and gambling business. I'm certain now more than ever that they also dabble in human trafficking. They were so willing to do it to me that they'd totally be cool with selling someone who isn't family.

I wipe away the tears that fall unwillingly down my face when I think about my fate.

Unwilling—like everything in my life.

I'd never let him see me cry, but the moment he's gone, I let them pour down my pink, tear-stained cheeks. I'm not sure if he'd laugh or get angry if he came back, but he won't even bother to come back. He's done what he came to do and that's it.

I hate my husband with a passion so great I can barely make it through the day. Hate is an understatement of epic proportions. I want him dead, and I'd do it myself, but I don't have anywhere to run if I killed the bastard. I have no money, no friends, no family, and would create more enemies than I can count.

Did I ever really have a family? They threw me to the wolves, selling me out for pennies on the dollar.

A life for leniency.

A life for ties to more power.

They didn't get the power, and I got a man who hate-fucks me like a used-up whore who disgusts him so much that he can't finish half the time.

His reaction to me is insane because as far as I've ever known, I'm considered a prize, beautiful compared to the most gorgeous women in Hollywood, but my husband doesn't treat me like he won a prize. Instead, he lives like he suffers every second in my presence.

The bastard has way too many allies and enemies in this world. Unfortunately, I'm not allowed to leave the house and meet his enemies. Hell, I haven't met his friends either. Our wedding was one of formality. There was no fanfare or massive ceremony for all to see. We signed papers in a courthouse with just our parents present.

The only people besides the main house staff that I've met are his parents. I'm betting that's the way they want it so he can get away with the abuse and so they know I can't turn on them. However, they have no idea that a really sharp kitchen knife would turn me into Michael Fucking Myers in a heartbeat.

Rafael also has an older brother Santino that no one in the family will mention in front of me. He's currently in prison for the murder of a public official, but that's all I know about him. They act like they shouldn't be proud of their boy. After all, murder's nothing new to them and not a disgrace. Maybe it's the fact that he got caught.

I quietly pull the pillow out from under my ass and slide off the bed to stand so they can't hear me. His release runs down my leg, but it's better than being anywhere near my womb. I shiver in disgust. Why did my dad make that arrangement? Why did he force me into marrying this asshole? Nothing like a marriage between two mafia families to strengthen a truce. Now I'm stuck with a man whose throat I'd love to slit.

I can't take a shower yet because his men literally sit outside my door to hear if I do. He wants me pregnant and having his heir. There's family unrest. I don't know why he just doesn't legitimize the little baby he has with his mistress. The boy is about two years old, from what I've heard.

I'm more than happy for them to do that than sleep with the fucker ever again. Then again, he likes that I hate his touch. He wants me to be his unwilling wife. He gets off on the abuse. I grab the sheet and walk to the bathroom.

Using a douche, I squirt out as much of his seed as I can. I don't flush so they can't hear me, but then I set the bottle back into the supposed hair dye kit that I've never used. I'm not doing it just to stop from getting pregnant, but also I want nothing to do with him and that includes his weak release.

Another shiver runs through me. Damn, it's warm out. Why am I so damn cold? I have a feeling I'll have my period in a couple of days, which will definitely warrant a beating.

I walk back to my bed and lie down, pretending to be resting just in case they do a surprise check-in. I sigh and cover my eyes with my forearm.

I'm locked away in my gilded cage. The room itself is absolutely stunning and looks like the room of a concubine or harem, but I'm not even his love slave. I'm an obligation. He only comes in here for one thing and once he's done, he's gone, and I'm trapped and disgusted.

I have only one ally in this, and it's his lovingly wonderful mother. She's been sneaking me birth control since my engagement. It's the best gift I could have gotten, and I can't even express how much it meant to me when she slipped them to me.

I remember her words as clearly as the day she said them. "I don't want you to be in my position, but we have no choice. Here. At least this will give you a chance to one day get out." I cry thinking about the pain on her face. She may present a gentle, happy matriarch, but as someone in the same spot, I can read her like a book.

Over the months, we shared brief conversations and I learned that she didn't marry for love. Her hand was forced, just like mine. There's more to that story, but I haven't been able to ask. We're never given too much time alone, and I'm sure that's because they know she feels sympathy for me.

I pray they never learn of the pills. She has a connection that gave her a year's supply, which I keep in one spot that Rafael won't search. Not that he would. I'm not allowed to have anything. Everything is brought to me.

The timer goes off and I hop off the bed to wash up, but the bright light from the sun beams through the room and I have to drink it in. It's rare to get a great deal of sun at this time of the year.

The weather is warming up, but this is the northeast. Spring storms are always on the way in from the ocean. It's the start of spring, which usually means renewal, a fresh start, but to me it means a little more freedom to roam the gardens and plant. Of course the security is tight, but I can at least pretend that I'm a wife of leisure and completely content with my life.

I open the curtains to the balcony doors. They're locked for my protection, or so they claim. In reality, it's about stopping me from taking a nosedive into the cement below. Some days I've considered it, but I'd rather take Rafael with me. I won't make my death easy for him.

As I stare out, I can see movement coming from the left in front of the large portico. A black-on-black SUV pulls up and the driver exits to open the back door.

"Speak of the devil, and he shall appear." I see Rafael straightening his suit jacket before heading to the open vehicle door. He pauses and looks up. I quickly close the drapes so he doesn't see me. I know that it isn't a last glance out of love, but to make sure I don't try to leave.

If only I could call the cops or maybe the Feds, but I'm not sure who to trust since so many are in their pocket.

Then again, if they have them paid off, why is their oldest

in prison? I feel like there's so much more there that interests me. Something about Santino Marchetti has intrigued me since I first learned of him. When we became engaged, I remember thinking that his brother should be the one my parents sold me to. After seeing his picture, I would rather have been his wife because at least he was good-looking.

For the first week of our marriage, I would pretend that Rafael was his brother. It's stupid because they're nothing alike in looks, but it helped me cope with the situation. It ended when he heard me call him Santino when we were at dinner. I played it off because someone had said his name during the dinner.

It's the only reason I managed to walk away unscathed that night. After all, the house isn't full of pictures of the older brother. The only one I saw is the one they keep on the mantle, and I never look at it for more than a glance just in case their eyes land on me and see my curiosity.

I don't know why, but I can't stop thinking about Santino. Sometimes, I still fantasize about him like somehow he'd save me from this life. I shake my head and walk into the bathroom and turn on the shower.

As I'm washing my hair, I remember why. This morning, I heard the guard say something to Rafael before he came into my room and Santino's name was the only thing I could make out.

My shower's quick because I don't trust the guards. They don't have the go-ahead to take me, but that doesn't mean they don't like stealing peeks at me naked. I wrap a towel around my body and one around my long, dark hair.

Opening my closet, I pull out a pretty yellow top with a pair of jeans. My wardrobe consists of mostly the clothes that my parents bought as a wedding gift. I'm in the middle of brushing my hair when there's a knock.

The door unlocks and he waits for me to open it. I keep my body behind the door so he doesn't have a chance to ogle me. "Signora Marchetti, you're being summoned by Signor Marchetti," his guard informs me. I hate every single one of them.

Their eyes have roamed over me like I'm nothing but an object. They've already hinted that the second I give the boss an heir, I'll be their "cum dump" as they put it, and apparently, Rafael approves. What kind of husband would allow that?

"I'm allowed out of my cage. So thoughtful. Should I get dressed, or would his majesty prefer I go looking like a used hooker?"

"Please be presentable. Santino is here. Signor Marchetti temper's high. Do your best to check your attitude. If you don't, I'll inform him of your mouth."

"The prodigal son has returned. Am I supposed to service both of them now?"

"Well, he's been without pussy for a couple of years, so maybe Rafael will be lenient and let him do you in the ass. Something he's probably used to in the joint. Now get ready. I'll be waiting."

"Maybe they need to be made aware of your mouth, you little pissant." I dismiss him with a wave of my hand and close the door.

I fetch one of the four outfits suitable for the old bastard who makes my skin crawl and his oldest spawn. I double check my appearance. I tell myself it's because I'm trying not to get a beating, but in reality, something is demanding that I look good for Santino.

"Get out here now. Quit being a spoiled bitch. Signor Marchetti said to make it quick."

"What?" I throw open the door, ready for a battle with

this bastard. "Who the fuck do you think you are talking to?" I remind him.

"You are lucky that I don't have something sharp besides my tongue or you'd be gasping for your last breath." I flip him off and walk downstairs in front of the bastard goon. Reaching the closed double doors to the sitting room where they are waiting for me, I stop in my tracks.

Turning to the hired help, I grab his lapel and lift my knee, striking him right in the balls. "Speak to me like that again, and that's the least I'll do to you."

Straightening my clothes, I open the door and come face to face with my father-in-law who's opening it at the same time.

"You summoned me?"

He gives me a warning glare to keep myself in control. "Please come in and hold your tongue," he whispers the last part.

That means Santino doesn't know I'm a prisoner. In the corner of the room, a man standing about six three with broad shoulders in a nice suit is staring at the wedding photo of Rafael and me. He sets it down and then turns.

"Santino, I would like you to meet your sister-in-law, Giada." Hearing his name makes my heart jump.

Our eyes meet, and I sense a shift in the room.

Chapter Three

Santino

"Thank you all for staying on this whole time. I'm grateful for all your trust and support during that dark time. I'll be in and out today, but I ask that you keep my whereabouts a secret unless told otherwise. The threat on my life might be a possibility, so I must offer you an option. You can stay and I'll increase your pay, or you can leave. I ask, though, that you make the choice with careful thought. I will not be giving second chances. I need to know that I can trust those in my home."

There are four staff members: Martin, my personal assistant, my butler, Jasper, my driver, Joey, and Rita, my chef.

"You know I'm not going anywhere you aren't, boss," Joey says.

I knew that would be his answer. I nod and wait for the other two to respond. They look at each other and quickly back to me.

"We're not going anywhere, sir," Jasper and Rita say

together. They've been married for the past twenty years and have been great employees since they came to work for me three years ago. The point of keeping them on is also to learn who talks to my enemies.

Everyone leaves my office, but Rita comes back ten minutes later to collect the plate of eggs and sausage she brought in this morning. I completely forgot about it. She huffs as she glares at the plate and then softens her expression before looking at me. "Sir, your breakfast is getting cold."

"Sorry, I'm not hungry." With everything going on, I don't have an appetite. Besides, I've had a liquid breakfast this morning as I steel my nerves.

Rita seems put out, but I don't have to eat if I don't want to. I give her a look that says it's not up for debate. Before I might have let it go, but after spending a long time having people tell me what to do, I'm not going to let them start with me now.

"Very well. We need some dogs to feed the wasted food to." She grumbles all the way out of the room.

"That sounds wonderful. Two Dobermans would be great," I shout before she closes the door. That's something I should have thought of doing as soon as I got out of prison.

She pops back into the room, setting the plate down again. "If you're serious, I'll look into it." She smiles brightly, rubbing her hands together.

I pointedly stare at her and say, "Dead serious."

"Okay. I'll start looking around. Anything else in particular regarding the dogs?"

"I prefer young adult Dobermans if possible. Female or male doesn't matter to me." She's grinning from ear to ear and looks giddy, as if I told her that her food was the best I've ever had.

"Fantastic. I'll get on it." She leaves the room with an air of enthusiasm that is hard to not share, but the dogs are a stark reminder that my father and brother have a debt to me that's long overdue.

I call Joey. "Joey, prepare to depart in twenty minutes." I end the call as soon as he says yes. I need some time alone. It's funny that that's all I've had in my cell, but instead of resenting it, I find it helps me think. Solitude is my fondest friend.

I sit back in my leather, handcrafted chair from Italy and stare into space, thinking about the time that has passed. I'm thirty years old now, having let my golden birthday pass in prison with nothing more than a happy birthday from those who feared me or kissed my ass, figuratively.

The little debate I just had with my Rita reminds me that I'm back in the free world. I don't take orders, I give them. The world is my oyster, as they say, but I'm not looking into the distant future with plans that don't include a whole shitload of retaliation and retribution.

I roll the glass around, swirling the amber liquid. It's only eleven in the morning, and I'm already on my third drink. I can't make this a habit, but I have to gain control and muscle down my hatred in order to get to the people I need to get to.

I have a game plan full of strategy and time. I want my moves to be calculated and unsuspecting. There's no way I want to be caught before my revenge is had.

I check my watch again for the third time, tossing back a long swig of cognac while staring out of my office window on the second floor of my home. I should be outside, enjoying fresh air, but despite being locked up, I had gotten sunshine and fresh air every single day.

I worked my body to the bone day in and day out,

getting strong and ready. Ready to send someone to the grave.

My first full day back in the real world and I'm already itching to get a one-way ticket back in. Years, two fucking years, I'd been behind bars like a fucking animal. I want the head of the bastard that put me inside with a burning passion so strong that I can't think of anything else.

I slam the glass down on the three-hundred-year-old wooden desk that had belonged to an Italian count before I purchased it at an auction right before I ended up with my freedom taken away. The sound reverberates through my ears.

Damn. I still remember the sound of the gavel hitting the wooden base and the prison bars slamming closed. That was what happened when a man stayed clean instead of giving in to the natural order of things. I'd been put away for a murder I didn't commit.

Even with the truth out, I'm certain that many will still believe that I'm a hitman for my father's organization disguised as a wealthy businessman.

Time to go meet with my father and decide his fate along with everyone else in my family. I denied the life of crime only to let them suck me into a world where my name was dragged through the mud.

I don't know how many of them were involved and if it went all the way up to my father, but I know he resented my choice to leave the family to live on the legal side of the law enough to send me to prison.

A knock at the door drags my attention from the window.

"Come in," I say, standing and gearing up to leave.

Martin, my oldest ally, enters and says, "Signor Marchetti, your car is ready."

"Thank you, Martin."

In a moment of solemnness, he says, "It is so good to have you back." I nod and shake his hand. Martin has been one of the few who spent his time working to free me. He and my lawyer made quick work of getting me out, although people would see two years a long time; I sure as fuck did.

However, when it came to the court system, that was just a blink of an eye. I slip on my sunglasses and walk out to the waiting car, a blacked-out black sedan, with Martin at my side.

"I don't mean to push, but do you think you should go to see them alone?" Martin's one of the few people I trust, and he's one of the only people who know that the setup was an inside job.

"I'll be fine. I'm not alone. Plus, they don't know that I know the setup came from someone inside the family, and I doubt Diego would let slip that he ratted out Rafael." I won't be visiting again unless it's to deliver my revenge.

"Okay, but remember that you're to remain composed. Don't let on that you know." I smile because he's serious, as if somehow I'm going to forget my plan. I've been waiting two years to strike down all those involved, and none of them know I'm coming for them.

"I won't. I'm going to talk a little shop and see what's going on. I do have a call with my board of directors tonight so two hours after my arrival, send a text to remind me."

"I will. Be careful, please." He's afraid that my release was expedited so that they could time my death to their schedule.

I slide my tall frame into the back seat, popping the button on my suit jacket and adjusting it to get comfortable. It's been two years since I've worn a nice suit. I loved a quality-cut suit. All of mine were custom made and thankfully, Martin came in and took my measurements when they learned I'd be getting out and had my tailor working overtime to get me two suits by my release day and a dozen within the next week.

I take off my sunglasses and lower the divider to talk to my driver and friend. Sitting in a sixty-thousand-dollar car with Italian leather seats should feel like heaven, but the burning rage in me made the world hard to enjoy.

"Joey, take me to my parents' home."

"Yes, sir." I love being Italian and everything that it means, or at least what it used to mean, but nothing is better than loyalty, even if my right-hand muscle is Irish. He has his own code of ethics and family. I trust him with my life.

Hiring Joey was an easy choice because I secured his loyalty after saving his ass, literally, from some boy-pussy-hungry inmates. They never fucked with him again.

Despite knowing Rafael and someone else in the family betrayed me, I refuse to be anyone else's pawn. Big, hardened, and strong as fuck, I proved my street credit in prison while still remaining calm.

My goal is still to return to my clean life, but I have a few bodies to drop and then it's all clear from there. Finding those I can trust to take out the trash has been few and far between.

The drive from my home in Scarsdale, New York to Greenwich, Connecticut takes longer than I'd hoped, but I'm just in time to see my asshole brother drive away. Good. I don't want them together. I want uncoached answers when I speak to them about my imprisonment.

We pull up to the gate after Rafael's a good distance away. "We're here to see Mr. and Mrs. Marchetti," Joey says with his extremely thick Boston accent.

I roll down my window and smile at Anthony. My

father's main guard is completely surprised to see me, but he doesn't let on whether it's a good thing or not.

Gathering himself, he says, "Signor Marchetti, your father and mother will be so pleased to see you." He opens the gate and lets me in. We take the quarter mile up the driveway quickly, hoping to keep him off kilter. Seconds after we put the car in park, my father comes to the door, but it's my mother who comes running past him. She moves faster than I ever remember with a smile so wide it takes me by surprise and I smile too.

"Mi figlio mio. Mi sei mancato." She hugs me tightly. I can sense the pleasure and fear in her eyes.

"I missed you too, Mama." I kiss the top of her head.

"Come inside, the both of you," my father whispers his command harshly, looking around nervously as if someone's going to take us out. I don't know all the details of what's going on, but he looks scared.

"He can wait there," my father says pointedly referring to my driver. I nod to Joey. I'll let him have that little bit of upper hand if he thinks it'll help. Joey can drop every single one of my father's men in a matter of seconds.

Looking around at all the guards and then up at my father, Joey says, "Are you sure, boss?"

"Of course, Joey. I'll be back soon." He nods with a smirk. I know he's not going to sit there wasting his time. I give an discreet tip of my chin to him, and then I walk up the stairs, holding on to my mother's hand.

My father claps my face, kissing my cheeks. "I have missed you, my son. You have grown a lot in the past two years." His words are hollow, but I don't let on that he's not giving an Oscar-worthy performance.

"I'm so glad they were forced to let you go. I'm sorry I couldn't be there, but I won't risk your mother's life." God, how I survived living here is a damn surprise.

"Thanks. It's good to be free," I remark with a smirk. My goal is to play the grateful son. "Have you learned who set me up?" I question the second we're through the front doors.

"I have not. I have men looking into it, but it seems they've covered their tracks well. I'm not putting it past the Avanti family." There were some things I learned in prison, and some things I learned growing up. One was when my father was lying to me, and he's doing it right now. That pisses me off more than I thought it would. Is he covering for my brother, or does this lie directly at his feet?

After what I learned, he's had to live with the kid he didn't create. I look at my mother, and I doubt she could cheat on him. Hell, he would have killed her for that alone. I wish I could ask her today. My mother wasn't allowed to visit me in prison without my father, and that visit only came once because it was a hassle to get to the prison. Her letters were always sweet but vague because I'm sure he read through them before she sent them. One thing I'm going to do is set her free if he's had anything to do with my imprisonment.

"Please come in. There's much you have missed," my mother says. The warmth from her smile takes the edge off my revenge. I know her heart is good. It's always been that way despite my father's intentions to destroy the goodness in her. Maybe it was payback for all of his betrayals.

"Where's Rafael?" I ask, knowing that he just left.

"He had some business to attend to, but you know he's married. You have a sister-in-law now," my father says with a tinge of gloating in his voice. I can't wait to meet the whore he chose for his wife. She'll be on my chopping block too.

"Wonderful." I can't contain the annoyance. I know they wanted me to meet and eventually marry one of the daughters of the Avanti family, but that was when I broke off from the family and a few days before I ended up in cuffs, so he ended up with her.

"Don't be like that. She's a sweet girl." She swats my arm, scolding me like I'm a child. Something about that genuine feeling gives me the warmth that I didn't know I was missing. It's so wonderful to see my mother again. If she's a good girl, then my brother has probably ruined her. If she's sweet, she's stupid for getting involved with Rafael to begin with.

"Excuse me." My father briefly steps from the room and returns a moment later. "I've called for Giada to join us."

I look between them and make my apologies. "I can't stay long. I have much to do. My company needs my attention, but I had to come see you first."

"Please don't tell me you're leaving so soon." My mother looks as if she's going to cry, and it's the only thing keeping me here.

"At least stay for lunch. We were about to eat. Besides, there is some business I would like to talk to you about." He looks for the distaste in my expression, but I've learned a few tricks while incarcerated.

"Sure. Sounds good. I have some matters to discuss as well."

"I will inform the cook," my mother says, leaving the room for a moment.

"My boy, it is good to see you, but I can see how you've been hardened. You are better than your brother and I ever were. Don't let the past get in the way of your happiness." He's a fucking liar and he does it so smoothly that if I didn't know better, I'd get caught up in his praise.

"Let us hope that the past stays that way," I say, biting my tongue and leaving out the part about how those who did this to me will pay, and how I know he's not my dad and that's a part of my past I don't want in the past.

"How about a drink?" He waves a tumbler toward me from his sideboard.

I put my hand up to refuse. "No, thanks. I haven't had more than a drink in two years, and I've had three today."

Before he can respond, my mother comes back into the room with a grin. "Okay. It's all set. The cook is thrilled you are here as well."

"Thanks, Mama."

My father's phone vibrates and he lifts his finger, asking us to give him a minute as he excuses himself. "Sorry, I really have to take this." I nod, letting him know I'm okay with this.

Once he's gone, she says, "You mustn't worry. Cook loves you and the food is safe."

"What makes you think I'm worried?"

She tilts her head the way a mother does when she knows better than you do even when you try to bullshit her. "I know you. No matter how angry and vicious you may be now, you'll always be my sweet angel. I love you so much. I only wish you had met Giada first."

"Why?" I grumble. Any woman that would marry my brother is good for nothing in my eyes. Unless it's to bend her over with five fucking condoms on. Shit. I don't want anything to do with my brother's leftovers. Never have and never will.

"Because your brother is not good to her, but there's nothing I can do for her." Each word out of her mouth rings of pain and regret.

I'm trying not to feel sorry for this girl, but the plea in my mother's eyes is hard to argue with. "It's a shame. She married him."

"It wasn't her choice." The tension in her voice tells me

that she probably didn't have a choice either when she married a Marchetti, but I want to hear that from her. Unfortunately, I'll never get her alone long enough to answer that question unless he's dead or in prison.

"Ah. One of those. Why didn't he marry that prostitute he wanted so much?" I'm starting to understand a little more about my new sister-in-law. The Avantis must have made a sweet deal unless Rafael had something on them because there's no way anyone would force their daughter to marry that piece of shit.

"Because your father doesn't approve, and the deal went well for the right price. You both deserve more. Here. This is their wedding photo." She hands me the framed photo and then takes a seat on the loveseat. I hold in my hands the image of the most beautiful woman I've ever seen, and she's married to my brother.

The features on their faces scream pure love. I hold the frame harder than I should, but I can't stop myself from the instant desire and pain at the same time. I take back every damn thing I just believed a minute earlier. My heart's thumping out of my chest.

I continue to stare at it as she comes back to my side and whispers, "If you get a chance, I want you to rescue her. Neither of you deserve the cards you were dealt. And her bedroom is your old one."

That immediately pisses me off. He purposely did that. We have at least fifteen bedrooms in this home, and he gave her the one that belonged to me so he could bang her in there. I'm so damn disgusted, I don't know if I can hide it.

"Relax, Mother. I will." In a whisper, I add, "Tonight."

She would have been mine had I not been locked up. I may not have wanted to be a part of the family, but I would have taken one look at her and knew our lives were meant to be spent together. Luckily, I'm facing the corner wall near the fireplace mantle where my father can't read my expression or see the arousal between my legs when he enters again. Thank fuck for the heavy wooden doors that let me know he's back.

"Ah, your mother showed you your brother's wife. Beautiful. She will bring many handsome children to the family." A burning pain engulfs my lungs as if I've been poisoned. I can't describe the acidic taste in my throat as I want to lose my insides, knowing he's been the one to make her come, the one to worship her beauty.

The thought of her carrying his baby instead of mine tears me up inside. We haven't even met, and I can't express how much I need her.

He probably takes her for granted as nothing more than a gorgeous piece of arm candy to show the world. Then again, maybe not. If she were mine, I'd hide her from the world so no one could steal her from me.

This is the first picture I have seen of her as if she's never been spotted out before even though people have been clamoring for one. She's fucking stunningly beautiful.

While I get my desire under control, I hear an angry yet very feminine voice outside, followed by a grunt. My father opens the door, but I can't even face her yet. She enters the room, and I use the reflection of another picture to steal a glimpse of her. My mind goes a million miles an hour as I think of ways to feel her under me.

Our eyes meet, and I know that I'm not the only one. A hint of surprise mixed with lust shoots from her caramel-colored eyes. It's wrong how badly I need to fuck her, and yet so right. Revenge will be sweet. *Now for proper introductions.*

Chapter Four

Giada

I'M COMPLETELY TRANSFIXED ON THE MAN BEFORE ME. His body is the complete opposite of his brother's. Hell, everything about his appearance is the polar opposite of Rafael. Well, except the fact that they're both criminals. That one fact cools my desire and reminds me that we're not alone.

Quickly, I gain control of my reaction before I give the wrong impression or maybe even the right one. Santino closes the distance in a quickened but elegant pace. Suddenly, I'm a little lightheaded. I steady myself and greet the prodigal son. "Mr. Marchetti, it's a pleasure to meet you." My heart's beating a million miles an hour. I'm surprised I manage to get any words out.

"The feeling is mutual, Giada." He reaches out and grabs my hand, bringing it to his lips like a perfect gentleman. It's the way they train them. They put up that front of a respectable man, but they are all ruthless. Not one of them is worth another breath, but I'll be glad to watch them all take their last gasp of air.

"Come, join us for lunch. Rafael had to take a meeting and will miss out, but I'm sure you are hungry after your morning activities." My asshole father-in-law's meaning is fully clear. He's letting everyone know, especially Santino, that Rafael fucked me before he left.

Controlling the flood of embarrassment coursing through me, I smile and politely decline. "Hardly. In fact, I find that I don't have an appetite." If I didn't feel dirty enough before, now I feel just foul.

"Nonsense, Giada. You will sit and eat. You'll need your strength while carrying the next family heir."

"You're pregnant?" Santino utters in barely disguised disgust. His reaction is the only thing stopping me from losing my shit. For some reason I want to reassure him that I'm not pregnant. I've only seen the one picture of him, and he's nothing like the man in front of me. He's handsome either way, but that smile I saw in that old photo doesn't match the man that's doing some wrong things to my heart. It's fear. Yes, that's what I tell myself. Nothing but fear and maybe lust.

"Not yet." I'm shocked and my heart dances when he releases a sigh of relief at that revelation.

"Soon. We hope." My father-in-law is trying to stick the point to Santino. I stand straight up and look away from Santino and remember that I'm a married woman even if I'm devastatingly unhappy.

"I'm sorry, but I don't know anything about your family."

"She's Avanti's youngest daughter." My father-in-law doesn't allow me to answer for myself, which is common. I feel like a six-year-old's puppet. They throw me around like a rag doll, have me married to Mr. Potato Head, and speak for me as they dictate my every move.

"How old are you, Giada?" He pointedly looks at his father, catching the way he's controlling me.

"I'm nineteen." I get out before I'm spoken for again. It pisses my asshole father-in-law off, and inside I do a little happy dance while maintaining a neutral expression on my face.

"A little young to be married, no?" Before I can find something to say, the maid comes in and alerts us that lunch is prepared.

Santino takes my arm and hooks it under his. "Come." My in-laws walk together, and he pulls out my chair for me. He pushes it in, and I could swear he sniffs my hair as he stands straight.

I need to ignore the way he sends a rush of excitement through me. It's wrong and futile. He's no different. I heard he would be locked away forever, but then I overheard Rafael say his brother had been falsely accused and the real killer confessed. There should have been a parade for their son, but the only one who cared was Signora Marchetti.

"So, Giada, how is life here in the family compound?" he questions, taking a bite of his salad. For a man who's been in prison, he's finding the meal unappealing.

"Wonderful." I lie through my teeth. Does he believe me? I stare at him wondering a lot of things that don't make sense to me. How can I want to run my hands over his taut jaw?

"Nice." I can't read him, but a cough from Signor Marchetti calls my attention. I turn to him and see a grimace that is subtle and yet says so much. I'm going to be in trouble.

"Son, what are your plans?" It's clear that he's trying to drag us out of our little trance. Damn it, I'm hoping that he doesn't tell Rafael.

"Well, I still have my company. Tonight, I deal with some transitions, but I'm back in the office come next week to run my company the way I've always wanted."

"That's great to hear. I'm surprised they were able to maintain your rights as the owner." I want to ask questions, but I'm not allowed to speak unless spoken to. I open and close my mouth several times, itching to hear him speak directly to me. Why am I doing this? I shouldn't even register his existence because he's no different than his father and brother.

My father-in-law takes a drink of his wine, then looks at me and then to Santino. "Do you know the D'Angelos have a daughter that would be perfect for you?"

"Are you talking about Suzette?" Signora Marchetti asks. I try to remain calm, but the vision of him marrying her only pisses me off.

"Yes, my dear." Immediately the pangs of jealousy hit me. I know who they are talking about. I knew her from before I married Rafael. She's beautiful and willing to bed anyone, including Rafael if he would have met her.

"I'm not interested," he answers after swallowing his bite of food.

"Why not?"

He steals a look my way before he says, "I'm not in the hunt for a wife. And I doubt the D'Angelos would take too kindly to me playing with their daughter."

"She's a whore anyway," I let slip.

I flinch, waiting for the venom to come from Signor Marchetti's mouth, but instead he just chuckles. "Yes, Giada is right. She wouldn't mind a little fun now that you've been locked away so long."

My mother-in-law looks at both men and scolds them. "Rafael, Santino, is this the talk you should be having at the table? You could have this talk later in private."

Stolen Wife

"Sorry, Mama," Santino apologizes. "I suppose prison has made me forget my manners."

"I apologize as well, my dear." He never calls her that. Is he only doing that because Santino's here?

The lunch is short and to the point. Santino's phone rings, but he doesn't answer it. Instead, he stands and says, "Thank you. I'm sorry, but I must go. There's a great deal for me to do. I have a meeting with the board shortly. Perhaps we can speak later, Papa." He bows slightly to me. "See you later, Giada." He bends down and kisses his mother's cheek and excuses himself.

As soon as he's gone, Signor Marchetti leans over the table and says, "If Rafael saw the way you drooled over his brother, you wouldn't be taking another breath. It explains why he keeps you locked away. You're no better than Suzette."

"I don't know what you're talking about and frankly, I don't care either. Your son is vile and so are you. I'd rather die than have Rafael ever touch me again with his little dick." I throw down my napkin, but I don't get to take another step before he comes around the table and slaps me across the face, sending me falling to the floor.

"You don't ever talk that way to me again. I'm not the guards." I clasp my hand to my face. My mother-in-law comes around the table and helps me up to my seat.

"Now eat your food. I don't want this going to waste. We waste enough on you as it is." I sit there in silence with my head down, refusing to speak to either of them. In my head, I've pictured several ways of killing him. My hand lingers over the butter knife a couple of times, but I think better of it.

After about ten more minutes of silence, he pulls out his phone to summon one of his men, then he tells me to go to my room. One of the guards comes and escorts me

37

out like I'm not a part of this family. I know I'm not, but it feels twenty times worse now than it did this morning.

Suddenly dying seems like a much more rational way to go. I don't know if I can handle any more of the abuse. The attack drained my will. When I look in the mirror, I see the damage. It's pretty bad. Rafael will only do worse once he learns why his dad struck me. It's going to take a pound of makeup and a week at least to hide this mark, if I live that long. Rafael shouldn't be back tonight since his mistress lives in New York. They live like a happy couple over there as if he doesn't have a wife here.

Thinking about it pisses me off. I'm over here, receiving daily abuse and all because they want a legitimate heir like DNA tests and marriages can't be arranged with a snap of their fingers. They wanted a virgin bride, like that mattered when they treat me so brutally. My head throbs, but I don't have any pain meds up here.

I try to lie down, but my skull and my hip ache. I hit the chair harder than I thought on my way to the floor. I walk over to the window and wonder if somehow it's best to jump. I open the curtains and the sun shines in. Squinting a few times, I let my eyes adjust. I'm not sure how long I stand there leaning against the wall, but soon I can see the change in the color of the sky as the sun turns it orange.

A knock at the door startles me and I drop the curtains. I don't even get a moment to open it when Signor Marchetti comes in. "You looking to jump?"

"What? Are you planning to push me?"

"Why would I do that yet? If you don't get pregnant soon, I can see it happening."

"Is there a reason that you're here?"

"It's my house. I can be wherever I want. I'm warning

Stolen Wife

you to stay away from Santino. I won't let him ruin my son's happiness."

I twist up my expression. So he really doesn't care for his oldest, which doesn't surprise me but instead saddens me. Did Santino grow up with this kind of abuse? Did he kill for his father to win his love and respect?

"I'm trapped all the time. I will probably never see him again. I'm sure if he shows up, you'll have me locked up. What you don't get is that I don't want him. He's just like you and your other son. He's handsome, sure, but since Rafael wants to pawn me off to his men after he gets me pregnant, I can't help but wonder if I can at least get a good-looking goon."

"What the fuck do you mean?"

"Hasn't Rafael bragged about how I'll be passed around to that bastard out there and his others after I produce an heir?"

"He wouldn't."

"Well, he sure as fuck threatens me with it every time he suffers through fucking me."

"That's not happening. I don't give a fuck how many mistresses he has, but you will not disgrace or disrespect him by whoring around."

"Good, that's the first thing you and I can happily agree on," I inform him. I feel a modicum of relief.

"Wonderful, then maybe I'll finally get some obedience out of you."

"Maybe a dog would be a better wife for him, then."

He grips me around the throat. "I may not let him pawn you off on anyone else but keep that shit up, and I'll fuck you up your ass so hard you'll be bleeding for weeks." He tosses me like his son did just this morning, and I'm more afraid than I have ever been. It's a threat I hadn't been expecting. He smiles. "And I'm sure I'll fucking love every minute of it." He licks his lips and then leaves the room.

My skin crawls at the thought of his hands on me. I can't take it anymore. There has to be a way for me to escape. I'm going to try to be on my best behavior and find my way out. I'd rather live on the streets of New York going from shelter to shelter or town to town as long as I can get away from this sick and twisted family.

A plan. That's what I need. Who can I get to help me? Fucking hell. I might have to seduce one of the assholes I hate so much, but hopefully it doesn't come to that. The house is surrounded by one of the strongest iron gates ever made, or at least that's what I'm told. It spans a half mile in perimeter and there's cameras all around the compound and a half a dozen guards at any time around the house. The cook goes out at least once a week to the store along with two guards so they can carry back the bags. It's always on a Wednesday at noon. It's the only time that the gate's consistently available. Can I get the cook to help? Maybe I can sneak into the trunk and then have her unlock it and I jump out while they're in the store. I'll have to ask Mrs. Marchetti if the cook is willing to assist me in escaping.

At this point there's not a single guard or staff member that I know of that's on my side. I don't need her to actually do anything but pretend that I'm not in the trunk and unlock it. That might actually work. Goodness, I can only hope.

A little sense of peace washes over me, and I go to my stack of books and pick *War and Peace* because I want my mind to shut off so I can fall asleep.

Chapter Five

Santino

I EXHALE A BREATH I HADN'T REALIZED I'D BEEN HOLDING as I walked to the front door to leave. Sunbeams peak through the panes that run from the floor to the top of the door frame.

I slip on my sunglasses to get a better view of what is going on outside. Nothing looks out of the ordinary, but still I need to be on my toes. Pulling out my phone, I read the message from Martin, reminding me of my meeting. Reluctantly, I tuck my phone in my pocket and open the front door. There's nothing going down, so that's good, but from the look on Joey's face, he's less than pleased with the wait. He holds the car door open while his suit jacket reveals his piece.

It's a struggle to leave that house without her. I try not to think about what my father said in there, but it's exactly what he intended for me to hear. Rafael fucked her this morning. Which means he's clearly aware that there's an attraction between us and that could be extremely dangerous for her. He'd love to destroy me and everything I love. Love…no, it's not love, just an insane, inexplicable attraction.

I want her out of that house tonight. As soon as I get in the car, Joey runs to the driver's seat and drives off.

Once we're on the main road, he starts talking. "There are around a half a dozen guys walking the perimeter. I never saw more than three at a time, but I remember their faces."

"Did they harass you?" I ask, pulling out my phone and running a few tests on the gadgets Martin had told me about last night during our drive back from upstate New York. They prevent anyone, including Google, from tracking my movements. It's completely a ghost phone. I'm going to need all the tools and more to get into the house and get her out, so I better get started.

He scoffs. "They asked me every question under the sun, but I told them to fuck off. I asked them since their job is to protect their family, why the fuck were they bothered by the driver for one of the family members?" That's why I brought Joey with me. He's a hardened guy with balls of brass. There's no way my father's men were going to get shit out of him.

"What the fuck did they say?"

"Nothing. They didn't have a response, and then finally they tossed out that weak bullshit about needing the background on all those who work for the family. I told them it took them fucking long enough to come up with that basic-ass reply and that I'd be informing you of it. If your father isn't involved, then his men are at the very least."

"Oh, he's involved. There's not a doubt in my mind." I think about the way he kept watching my reaction and interaction with Giada. The thought of him hurting her hasn't stopped running through my mind as we drive on.

"I've got your back for whatever you're planning to do," he says, looking through the rearview mirror.

"Good. Tonight. We take Giada from this house," I inform him.

"Wait? Your brother's wife?" He's staring at me like I've lost my mind.

"She's not his wife," I growl. The word sounds so damn grotesque to me that I feel it strike the pit of my stomach harder than any blow from a boxing match. "She's not, and don't ever say that shit again."

"Wow. Whoa. Sorry." Reading my emotions, he doesn't press the issue and continues to drive to my offices. I have to take over control of them before tomorrow or they'll remain in the hands of the board.

"I want to strike as soon as we can. I've lived here my whole life. I know every nook and cranny inside and out. Besides, I have a little help."

"Who?" He raises his brow with a smirk on his face.

"My mama." She gave me information that's exactly what I needed to get Giada into my arms. I'm surprised that my mother hasn't found a way to leave herself. After all these years, she sticks around. If she wants out, I'll take her with me as well.

The entire ride back into the city, I concoct my plan to extract Giada. It's going to take a small team to sneak in without being seen and bring her home. I send out a couple of messages and place a quick call.

We pull up to my office building and park in the garage. My sign is gone from the usual spot, but that's fine. I'll have that replaced tomorrow. When I get inside, there's a new guy at the desk. He looks at me and then back at

Joey, who gives off the hired-muscle look even in an expensive suit. "How can I help you?"

"By getting out of my way. This is my company."

"I've never seen you before. Do you have some ID?"

"I'm going to try and be civil with you because you're doing your job, but only this once." Looking to Joey, I pass him my leather briefcase. "Hold this." He takes it and then I pull out my wallet to dig out the ID and hand it to the guard.

"Oh, sorry, Mr. Marchetti. Please don't fire me," he stammers.

I tug on the cuffs of my dress shirt under my suit jacket and then look at his name badge. Leaning in, I lower my voice and say, "Jose, I'm not going to fire you for doing your job. I expect that diligence out of an employee, however now that we got that cleared up, I better not have a problem again."

"Not at all, sir." He's shaking as he allows me to pass, and rightfully so. I'm seeing red at the idea that no one in this building knows who I am. We take the elevator up to my main office floor and walk up to the receptionist.

"Mr. Marchetti. Welcome back! It's so good to see you," she says. I look at her name plate because although her face is familiar, I forget her name.

"Thank you. Are all the board members in the meeting room?" I ask Karen.

I remember her briefly starting right before everything went to shit. "All but two. They are calling in, though, Mr. Marchetti. Would you like anything to drink?"

"A bottle of water will do."

"Here you go," Joey says, handing back my case. I smile to myself and then up to him because of what's in here. They aren't going to like me.

"Thanks."

She walks to a nearby cooler and brings me a bottle. "Thank you."

I burst through the doors, hoping to catch them talking while I leave Joey outside of the conference room to watch the comings and goings of those in the office. My sudden release and arrival has probably taken them all by surprise. Most of them don't know if they'll have a job tomorrow. That's not my intention at all. I want my company to operate as it always has.

"Hello, I'm back," I cheer as all heads turn to me. Suddenly everyone stands up but one.

"Just in time," Glen Denton says, barely disguising his disappointment as he sits on his ass. I've always hated this fucker, but he'd been on the board before I took over this company. It takes a lot to get one of them kicked off, but I have an ace up my sleeve and I'm about to play it.

"Yes, I'm sure that you're glad I'm back, Denton. Now, everyone, sit. I don't have a lot of time. My life has gotten remarkably busy." I wait for everyone to take their seat before making my way over to my seat at the head of the table. Undoing my jacket button, I sit comfortably as if nothing has changed in two years. "I'm still the controlling owner, and I plan to implement some ground rules. My assistant, Martin Giuseppe, has created a draft handbook. I have to go over the details with the company lawyer, who will be meeting me tomorrow to do all of this. Please read these over. As the board, I'm giving you some options. I have appreciated that some of you have believed in my innocence."

"Some of us think you belong in prison."

"Well, then, you can resign from the board because you're a liability to my company. It was proven that I was not only wrongly convicted, but the real killer had been caught." Is he stupid enough to continue talking shit?

"Yeah, but that's just one of the many bodies you could be tied to." He's stupider than he looks.

"Really, Denton, please inform everyone of the information you have that I don't have." I'm going to bury this bastard one way or another. Financially seems like the best way for this sick fuck.

"Everyone knows who you're related to." I roll my eyes and check my watch. I don't have time for this, so I'm going to just toss him a little parting gift.

"Yes, but not everyone knows you're related to a child molester, do they?" Denton turns white as a ghost. "Yes, I know about him. I also know that the apple doesn't fall too far from the tree. You learn a lot of things in prison that you didn't have access to as a free man. I expect your resignation by the end of the day." The authorities have already been given the information and are keeping tabs on him right now. I've made a charitable contribution to an agency that deals with the victims of sick fucks like Denton. That's the extent of my involvement, though. I'm just trying to get my life back.

Denton stands up without looking at anyone but me. "You'll pay for this, Marchetti."

"I already have. Two long years. Trust me when I say that I'm done playing fair. Get out of my building before I have you arrested."

He storms out. Then I address the rest of the five members of the board and the two that are listening in. "Anyone else have a problem with me?"

A cacophony of "nos" go around the room. "That's what I thought. Now, let's get down to business."

I got a lot of reading done while in prison. Since I still owned the company and it couldn't be taken from me without giving me millions, I received all the materials for the meetings, copies of the contracts. I may not have had my freedom, but I had access to everything to make shit happen. Thankfully, I was smart enough to put a clause in there regarding imprisonment. With everything my family is involved in, I couldn't be too careful. My company staying afloat was the only thing that kept me from losing my mind in that small cell.

"Okay, so I see that the cost of timber has gone up with the brush fires that swept California this year. I suppose it was expected. What are your thoughts? Price increase or decrease in manufacturing." I own a multibillion-dollar legal timber mills and iron ore mining company. One of my professors in college hooked me up with a friend of his in Africa who helped me get started. When he died, he left everything to me with the hopes that I would expand and donate as well. I kept my promises on both ends, and now it's time to assess the company's direction and make the necessary changes to keep us relevant and competitive while maintaining best business practices.

The meeting lasts two hours. As that's happening, I check on my brother's location. He's in the Bronx with his mistress, or at least that's what I believe. I don't want to go home and find him in bed with Giada or I might slit his throat on the spot and forget my plot for revenge.

"Thank you all for taking the time to meet with me. I'm glad to be back and I'm ready to continue to make the company a success." While I stuff everything back into my case, I put a monitoring device underneath the table. My plan is clear. I want to hear everything going on in and around my business. At this point, I trust no one. I go into my office and slip on a pair of gloves to avoid leaving my own trace as I set up three hidden cameras in the office with both voice and audio. It takes me twenty minutes to go through my things and organize them the way I like. My office has recently been cleaned and aired out, but when I was first arrested, my office was ransacked and my personal belongings seized. Fucking Feds. I leave after grabbing a few things I need. After the weekend, I'll know a lot about who I can trust and who I can't.

As I open the door, I pull off the gloves and tuck them into my pocket. Joey's waiting on the other side, leaning against the wall facing my door.

"Ready?" he asks, tilting his head toward the elevator.

"Yes. Let's go," I say before addressing Karen again. "I'll be back on Monday." I don't have to do anything else in the office until then, especially because I'm betting someone sneaks into my office by the end of the day.

"Did you monitor the car?"

"Yes. No one has gone near it." We have cameras all around the building, and I made sure to watch for a slick play by anyone. I've never felt so damn paranoid before, but things have changed and they're going to get a lot worse before they get better.

"Great." As soon as we're in the car, I reveal our plans. "I've already gathered the team you want. We don't kill anyone. I want to be in and out with her. The cameras need to be down and the men out cold. The rest I can handle on my own.

It's well into the night when we put the plan into motion. My cell phone puts me in my home and my surveillance cameras are on a loop cycle using last night's footage. Now, we drive off to my father's estate with my best tech guy, Rogers, who hacks into my father's security system effortlessly. It's not the latest in tech because my father feared that his system could easily be hacked with all the cloud software and modern cyber techniques. My guy still managed to breach the system and keep the cameras facing away from my path to Giada.

"Are we ready?"

"Yes. We have a ten-minute window to get her out of there. That's about how long it will take for them to notice something's wrong with the system if they're smart. Twenty if they're stupid. Let's hedge our bets," my tech guy says.

The physician, who's a former mercenary, hands me a capped syringe. "Shoot her with this. It'll sedate her. The ass cheek is the best spot for this."

"She'll pass out in twenty seconds or less." I nod and take the syringe, setting it inside of my flak jacket.

"Got it." We bump fists and then two guys and I sneak in just in case we need to drop anyone. He's temporarily disarmed the sensors above the gate, so we easily jump down. There are no ground sensors. That's what my father said his men were for. It works and we're on the property. My men remain in the shadows out of the camera's view while I run across the lawn to the front of the house.

From my position, I don't pass by the front door and now I'm just under her balcony. Quickly and quietly, I scale the wall. I prepare the ropes for our descent back down. Then I pop the lock. I could use the key I have for it, but I don't want them to know it's me.

I creep inside the darkened room. On the bed is just one body and as I get closer, I see her sexy silhouette. God, my dick hardens instantly, not what I need at the moment, but I ignore the fucker because our lives depend on it. Slipping out the syringe, I uncap it and then climb onto the bed and brush my hand over her face as my other hand goes to her ass. She feels fantastic in that silky nightgown, but I'm immediately reminded that time is of the essence.

Still, I can't resist stealing a kiss. She moans into my

mouth, joining me, and then says, "Rafael." My hard-on is gone and in its place is jealous rage.

"Don't ever say his name in my arms," I growl out, hating that I'm already fouling up my own plan. With her, I truly have no control.

"I don't want you," she pronounces before the drug takes effect.

"Too bad." I kiss her forehead and scoop her off the bed. When I do, I spot something that sets me off. She's got a bruise almost the size of one side of her face. The anger in me drives me to move quicker to get us both to safety.

Sliding a harness around us, I wrap her legs at my waist and then lower us to the ground. Once that's all done, Joey's at my side, taking all the gear. He sees the bruise in the moonlight, and the realization that we may have been just in time strikes us both. I carry my treasure as I run past the cameras and over the wall. Jail sure as fuck paid off when it came to getting fit. I trained day and night to get fuller, stronger, faster, and more cunning each and every day inside.

The vehicle's waiting down the road and we all climb inside. I cradle Giada to my chest, wrapping her up with a blanket I have in the car so they can't see her dressed like that. "A minute to spare. Let's get out of here." After we're ten miles away, they drop the hack and allow the cameras to return to position and all sensors to resume normal operation.

"Damn, she's been roughed up," the doctor says.

"I wonder if your brother came back before we knew it and then left again. It's only a half-hour drive."

"I don't know, but I do know he's going to pay for this." I brush her hair away from her face while the doc takes a look at it. He touches it, and she moves slightly with a painful moan.

"Sorry. I'm looking for any broken bones, but it's just a really good wallop. Give her some ibuprofen for the pain. I'll come over to get blood work for her in two days."

"Good. I hope to hell she's not pregnant with that bastard's baby."

"She's beautiful, but she looks frail and a little malnourished, so there's a good chance she's not, especially if she's receiving beatings. Then again, you never know."

"We got your back either way."

"Thanks. I knew I could count on you."

"Take care of her. What about your mother? Are you going to try to get her out as well?"

"That's going to be a little harder. I don't know if she wants to leave. You know how it is. You stick with your husband no matter what. She came from Sicily engaged and married my father as soon as she landed."

"Oh, well. You should find out. Your mother's this girl's only ally."

"Until now," Joey adds.

"I second that. If she means something to you, she means something to all of us. I've got a little sister and if any fucker did that to her, he'd be missing all his fingers and his dick."

"Thanks." She moves a little in my arms, so I adjust and cradle her closer.

Once we're through the garage of the house, each guy watches for anyone lurking before I carry her up to bed. I can't have her lying in that shitty gown. She's mine, so I slide it over her head and slip on one of my tee shirts. I freeze and stare. She looks so damn sexy in my shirt and in my bed, but then I see the rings on her finger. Growling, I gingerly pull them off and slip them into my drawer. I might need them later. Then I tuck her in and then step back out to address the guys before I go to bed.

Doc and my tech leave together with plans to stop at a liquor store to give themselves an alibi. Joey goes down to his room, and Martin looks on. "Sir, I made arrangements for Rita to pick up some new clothes this afternoon. She claims she needed a new wardrobe. Nothing much, of course, but you know some women can shop," he says with a smirk, giving me three shopping bags full. "Oh, and it's all on her husband's account, so I'll give them cash in the morning."

"Fucking wonderful. Thanks. Now, if you'll excuse me, I need to be in bed just in case they come looking for her in the morning. I can't appear to have gotten no sleep."

"Perfect. I'll bring in breakfast around nine."

"Sounds great."

"She's got to be special, Santino."

"She is to me." I close the door and strip down to my boxers. All of my clothes will be dealt with in the morning, but for now, I need to hold her close to me. The bed dips as I slide under the covers with her, pulling her close.

It's going to be a rough couple of weeks before I even begin to seduce her. Shit, I don't even know if I still got it in me. It's been a long time, and I was a young man who didn't have to try to get a woman to fall for me. They fell at my feet just because of my name and looks.

For Giada, I'm sure that's going to be the opposite. She probably sees me as an extension to the life she has had to this point. I'm going to change that no matter how long it takes because she's mine, even if I have no real idea where to start. This abduction had been a last-minute priority and nothing else had been planned. I'm grateful for Martin's quick thinking and actions because I hadn't considered the clothes aspect and I sure as hell can't let her out until I get Rafael out of the picture.

She rolls in my arms so her face is nestled against my chest. The soft sigh coming from Giada's lips reassures me that I did the right thing.

Chapter Six

Giada

I'VE BEEN IN MY BEDROOM SINCE SIGNOR MARCHETTI SENT me away after he slapped me. It may sound terrible, but I want to slice the old bastard up as soon as I can. I dread Rafael coming home to his father's proclamations and then he beats me again. So far he hasn't come back, and I wonder if he will. God, I wish I had a way to escape before he returns. My nerves are on edge.

Damn Santino Marchetti. He had to be insanely gorgeous and staring at me like he could eat me up. My body heats up thinking about the way he licked his lips at lunch, and it wasn't because of the food.

I picked up one of the how-to-be-a-mother books, but it doesn't help me fall asleep because my mind hasn't stopped running on overdrive. I read it for the first time, and I picture myself holding a beautiful baby boy in my arms as my husband slides his arms around me from behind. "Ugh," I grumble, slamming the book on the bed.

I can't read this because it's not Rafael—it's Santino as my husband. Daydreaming is stupid and pointless.

Jumping off the bed, I change into a silky nightgown and pop my birth control. I stare at the remaining packets, wondering what would happen if I took them all at once. Can you OD on them? There's no way I would know. I have access to nothing but a few books in my room that are beyond depressing. My prison is an iron cage dusted with gold leaf.

If I weren't already on the pill, I'm sure he would have beaten a child out of me. I'm on the last active pill for the month. The next week is my placebo week and then my period will come, which means my ass better find a way out of this house before I get it because they will probably kill me if I'm not pregnant.

I listen at the door, hoping that I don't hear anything. My guard usually leaves the floor around nine. It makes no sense why they bother because I can't leave on my own. The entire compound is surrounded by guards, and I can't climb. It's probably a skill I should learn. I pick up *The Grapes of Wrath* and dig in. Every page I struggle to make it through causes my eyelids to dip lower and lower until I've fallen asleep.

It's dark when I'm startled awake by a noise, but I don't move. I hear the footsteps creeping closer to the bed, and I pretend to still be asleep. I don't want to consider the plan Rafael has for me. The bed shifts with his weight and I feel his hand come up to my face, I brace for it, but he doesn't move to my throat. Instead, he slides his mouth over mine as he lightly pinches my ass. I can't believe the way I'm moaning into his kiss, loving his mouth on me. What the hell? He's my bastard husband. Rafael?

"Don't ever say his name in my arms." I swear I hear Santino's voice as my world darkens.

"I don't want you," I utter as I pass out.

I wake up groggily with my head fuzzy, but from the looks of it unharmed. Maybe last night had all been a dream. Did I really dream about Santino kissing me? I'm glad Rafael didn't come in and hear me if I did. I roll over onto my back when I hit a large frame. A frame much larger than Rafael's. I reach out and feel a muscular chest. I open my eyes and see Santino with his elbow propping him up as he looks at me.

"Good morning." The smile on his face almost makes me forget the danger we're in.

"Good morning? Are you nuts? What are you doing in my bed? Rafael will kill you. Oh my goodness. I wasn't dreaming." My heart's racing as fast as my mind is. I can already picture Rafael and his goons busting down the doors and shooting up the place on principle alone. Or maybe they'll just torture us to death. I look into his eyes and all I see is mirth, which pisses me off as much as it turns me on.

"You thought you dreamed of me, baby?" He slides his hand over my hip and under my nightgown. My skin tingles from the gentle grip he exerts. God, how am I getting turned on?

It makes me mad how hot he is, and I become flustered with his touch. I shove his hand away and glare at him. "That's not what I meant."

"It doesn't matter. You're not in your bed at the compound. You're in our bed in my home."

"What?" I flip around and look. This isn't my room. The room is made of clean lines, greyish-blue walls with a large television mounted to the wall. I'm confused and taken aback by this. Slamming my eyes shut, I take several deep breaths and then pinch myself.

"You're not dreaming. I took you, and you're here. End of story." He sits up in the bed, and it's the first time I notice that he's ripped from his shoulders down to his…oh my goodness. He's extremely hard right now. I turn to look away. "Are you hungry?"

"I'm not sure," I respond with a barely audible whisper. My confusion has only grown. I stand to get some space between us and then it dawns on me that I'm not in my nightgown anymore. Instead, I'm in a big tee shirt with my hard nipples pressing against the letters.

"You took off my clothes? Are you trying to get us killed?" I cover my chest, like it does me any good. The man took off my clothes last night. Did he do anything else to me?

"I'm not afraid of any of them. And yes. Do you think I'd let you wear something my brother probably has fucked you in? I don't want anything of his tainting my home." I'm seeing a change in his mood. His temper's slipping past that cool, calm, sexy façade. It's as if my heart's breaking, which makes absolutely no sense since I've never had a chance for love to come and tear it apart.

I glare at him and test his actions. I have to know who I'm dealing with. "Well, then, I should go, since I'm his." He jumps off the bed and crosses the distance between us. Unable to stop myself, I flinch, waiting to feel the sting. He's much larger than his brother and father, and I know this will hurt more, and not only physically.

"I'm not him and you're not his," he growls, dragging me with one arm around my waist and the other in my hair. His mouth slams down on mine. God, that kiss had been real. Before I can melt into him, he pushes off of me.

"That was wrong," I say as I watch him get dressed.

Santino slips on a white undershirt and a pair of grey dress slacks before sliding on a crisp white dress shirt.

He turns around to face me with the shirt still wide open. I'm amazed by the feral look in his eyes. From head to toe this man is perfection, but his mouth on mine was the most insanely sexy thing in the world I've ever experienced.

He stalks toward me, but this time I don't flinch because I'm ridiculously hoping for another kiss. He tips my chin with his thick thumb, pulling my bottom lip from under the grip of my upper teeth. "Felt fucking right to me." My body heats up and I breathily look up into his eyes that are trained to my lips, waiting for more. Instead, he steps back and says, "Now, if you'll excuse me, I have a call to make. Please eat." He points to the trays on the table that's in the middle of the room.

"So you're going to leave me up here locked away?" I ask, changing one cell for another.

"Damn right," he growls, nodding his head as he grabs his phone and gun.

"You're just like your brother." It's out of my mouth before I can think about it. I'm sure that is going to set him off, and then I'm going to feel his wrath. God, it would break my heart if he hit me. I should be used to the abuse, but when I see him, I don't know why I fear his brand of evil.

He stands by the door with a smirk on his face. "Sweetheart, I get that you want to fight me. Test me. I get that you want to believe whatever lies you tell yourself, but deep down you know I'm nothing like my brother, and soon you'll know that in more ways than one." He leaves me alone, locking the door behind him.

"Bastard." I sit on the bed. A part of me is secretly happy to be away from Rafael and his father, but what does Santino have planned for me? Does he want to fuck me too? Of course he does. That hard-on and the way he kissed me…whew, nothing but pure, lustful fire. But could I be reading this wrong? Is this some sort of revenge? Why should I even care?

I tuck my hair behind my ears, feeling the sting of the bruise. Damn, it's painful. I take a deep breath and get a whiff of the breakfast on the table, making my stomach become a rumbling engine. Walking over there, I lift the lid to eggs, bacon, sausage, and homemade hash browns. I don't think I've had a meal like this in forever. I help myself to a small serving because even though it smells incredible, I don't get to eat often or anything hearty, so I don't want to get sick.

The first bite of the bacon hits the sweet spot in my palette, and I release a moan. The food is too good to be true, but I only eat a little more because I'm feeling a little lightheaded. Oh God, please tell me he didn't poison me.

I take a deep breath, and I'm okay again. So it's just my paranoia, it seems.

I step into the bathroom to freshen up and to examine my father-in-law's handiwork. The bathroom is large and made for a man like Santino. Everything is new, but then again the man spent years in prison, so this is all newly added, I'm guessing. I run my hands over the granite countertops, feeling the cold stone against my fingers, and yet I feel the warmth of this place. Then I finally look up and see my reflection. The bruising from yesterday has darkened so it matches the pain that's radiating from it. I can't believe how terrible it looks.

"I could kill him for that alone." I turn to the door and see Santino leaning on the door jamb. He straightens up and moves toward me. The way his body moves, I feel hypnotized. There's power in every step.

I face him and feel almost obligated to tell him the truth about this, so I do. "This wasn't Rafael's efforts."

"Who?" His teeth are clenched as he grits out the word. I can see he already knows but needs to hear it from me.

"Your father."

"What? Why?" He's angry, and that strangely makes me comfortable to tell him what happened.

"As soon as you left, he threatened to tell Rafael that I was flirting with you, and I got a smart mouth with him. For an old man, he's still extraordinarily strong."

"He's lived long enough." The gruff words hit my ears and my pussy's flooded. This man has a way about him that draws me in like a moth to a flame. It's dangerous, and yet I have a hard time fighting the urge to step into his path and demand he show me what I'm missing.

"It's not your problem. I'm only glad I'm away from them. I am away from them, right? You're not going to send me back there, are you?"

"Never. Over my fucking dead body are you returning to them."

"Thank you. I don't care why you took me last night, but either way, I'm temporarily safe from Rafael."

"Soon it will be permanently," he says to himself.

"What's that supposed to mean?" I ask when it strikes me that he's going to kill his brother. I'm not against it, but why would he want to do that?

A knock at the door stops him from answering. He presses a finger to my lips and then walks to get it.

I creep to the bathroom door, attempting to hear the exchange. "Sir, your lawyer is downstairs waiting for you. I set him in the living room."

"Any word?"

"Nothing. It's still quite early. They may not even know

she's gone yet." I'm nervous to see what happens when they realize I'm gone.

"True. Very well. I'm looking forward to his reaction when he learns the truth. Revenge will never be sweeter." I hold back the gasp and wait for Santino to walk back in.

"I want you to stay up here and don't move. You can watch television. Those bags of clothes are for you. I don't know what's in them, but I'm told it should be everything you need." The formal, stiff tone turns my body icy cold.

He leaves me there standing in the middle of his bedroom with tears welling up in my eyes. I'm just a pawn. *Okay. Fight these feelings. I don't care if he can make you come on a dime or if his stare makes your heart hope for a happily ever after. The first chance you get, you take it.*

I grab the bags and spread them out on the bed. Everything is from Target, which doesn't surprise me. Rafael was the same way. Expensive things for him, nothing for me. It's not that I don't like Target clothes, but I expected more for some reason. God, I have to get it out of my head that he wants something more. I'm descending into madness.

After picking out a cute white tee and a pair of pink cotton shorts, I grab the nude bra, which is way too small for my chest. Shit. The panties will do simply fine, but since I'm trapped in this room, what does it matter if I have a bra?

As I pick up the rest of the clothes and toss them in the bag, I catch the faint aroma of his scent. Like a fool, I lie back down in the bed and bring his pillow to my nose. It's so captivating that I lose track of time and all my worries.

Chapter Seven

Santino

"Dimitri, it's so good to see you again." I welcome my longtime friend with a one-armed hug. He warned me before they played me that he hadn't trusted my family, but no, I didn't want to listen to him. I've had to live with that for the past two years, and he's made sure to remind me of it on numerous occasions.

"Same to you, Santino. You're looking good." I should say the same to him. I was too preoccupied at the courthouse to notice, but he's looking stronger and his grip isn't that of a weak lawyer but a man who has been hitting the gym frequently.

"Knowing I'd be getting my life back looks good on me, but shit, I could say the same about you. Have you been working out a lot more?"

He nods, but there's a sense of frustration on his face. "Yes. My acquaintances in Russia have been giving me a hard time about my refusal to work for them, so I'm preparing to go toe to toe with them if push comes to shove."

"I didn't know you had dealings in Russia." That's a revelation to me.

"It started out as a favor for my cousin Alexei a few weeks ago. One thing led to another, and here I am in bed with guys I don't want to have any dealings with and another boss of the Bratva out for my head."

"Do I need to be concerned?" It's not something I need on my plate right now. I'm ready to go to war with my family. Technically I've been at war this entire time, but this time I'm the one striking first.

"Nyet. They are sensible enough to leave my clients alone. This is strictly a family issue."

"Good, but I hope that we're more than just business associates," I remind him. There are very few people I can call my friends, and Dimitri is one.

"Of course. Of course we are. It's just not something they need to be made aware of. They'll steal your firstborn if you let it slip that you're having a baby."

"Fine. I'll be watching my back either way. Forget about everything else. We have so much to go over. Do you want some coffee?"

"I'd love some. It's been already a long morning." I summon Jasper and ask for some coffee. Once he leaves, Dimitri continues, "I've been down to the courthouse to get the papers processed. I believe there's something you need to know. While I was there, Denton came out of a stairwell, speaking to Antonetti."

"My father's lawyer?" Suddenly, my collar gets too damn tight. I loosen it and then stand up because coffee isn't going to be enough. "Do you want a drink? Because I'm having one."

"No on the drink, and yes, unfortunately, his lawyer.

I'm sorry, Santino. It's not something you wanted to hear, I'm sure. I don't know what they were talking about, but I did manage to take a quick picture on my phone."

He hands me the phone as Jasper comes back in with a cup of coffee each on a tray with cream and sugar. Dimitri takes it and adds some of both while I look over the photo, hoping to find something to give me answers. "Denton has a death wish or maybe I'll just toss his ass in prison. You do have all that information, right?"

"Yes, I do. Do you want it activated?" he asks and takes a sip of his coffee. "Damn, this is good."

"Thanks. Only the best after a long time with sludge." I take a drink of my whiskey. "Give it twenty-four hours. I want him to lead me to the rest of them. If he's dealing with Antonetti, then I wonder how long that's been going on."

"I don't know. Your father has been making sure to keep his nose out of everything that has to do with your arrest and every detail surrounding it, but he comes off too clean, especially with connections to the victim and the real hitman."

"I'm guessing the more he gets riled up, the quicker he'll make a mistake."

"Or get desperate. We have to be prepared for both." I'll be ready. The one thing I remember before going to prison is hitting up the shooting range and creating design patterns with my turn. I have marksman skills, which pissed my father off when I refused to bring those skills when he wanted them.

"And I am. I've played this chess match so many times in my head. I won't lose to him. I've smartened up about how dirty people can be."

"You need more people on this, but I know there's too much at stake for loose lips." He's right, but if we send anyone in to investigate, they have to be inside and there's no one inside the family that would let in a spy. I don't have loyalty like that from them because I'm the son that dared to dream for better. I'm the one who turned my nose up at violent crime and murder.

"Exactly." I already feel like my circle is too big, but I can't do without them and I trust each one of them implicitly.

"There are a lot of people that would love to bring your father and brother down, but so far all their dealings have appeared above board, even though you and I know that's not true."

"Just keep me informed. We both have copies of the evidence to put Denton away. I'm betting he'll talk, but they'll have a hit on him before we can get the details. Do you have anything on the Avanti family?"

"Besides that they are rumored to sell girls, I've heard of drug trafficking."

"Damn, then they have a lot to lose and won't play nice. I'm going to find a way to make my family turn on theirs." I may have already started that endeavor if they take the bait.

For the next three hours, we go over our strategy as well as my company legalities that need to be handled before I go into the office. My paternity is another issue that I'm sure Dimitri is looking into discreetly. Honestly, I want the answers from my mother. I deserve to hear them from her.

After sending him on his way, I find myself slowly creeping up the stairs and back into my bedroom. There's a lot I want to say to Giada, but for the time being, I just have to see that she's doing okay.

The bed has been neatly made and the bags are full on the bench by the foot of the bed. When I look toward the open bathroom door, I spot Giada examining her face. She's only wearing a pair of underwear and a tee shirt. I move to the doorway of the bathroom and lean against it to watch her. Groaning, I can see her nipples are pebbled and pushing against the fabric.

I could stare at her all day, but not like this. My brother didn't just fuck her. He beat her and so did my piece of shit father. God, that would kill me if he took her to bed too. That's more than I can even stand. It's killing me that she's in pain. There's no way it doesn't hurt like hell.

"You're back?" She doesn't turn to face me. Instead, she watches me through the mirror. I want to see the lust I saw the first time I met her, but she's scared of me.

"You sound surprised. I told you I would be." I rake my eyes over her form. From head to toe I catalog each spot and what I want to do to her. God, slipping behind her and sinking my hands onto her waist and thrusting into her pussy is all I want to do right now.

"What do you want from me?" Her voice is just a whisper, revealing her vulnerability. Something I didn't see before. I step closer, entering the bathroom, but I'm still far from her.

I look into the mirror, staring at her face, and confess, "It's complicated."

"I know this all has to do with Rafael." Her body stiffens up and I want to tell her it's not, but I can't lie and pretend that it isn't.

"Not all of this." She doesn't believe me, and it's written all over her face. The intensity of my desire for her is only matched by my hatred for him and the life he stole from me.

"When can I leave?"

My response is instant and final. "Never." The question sounds ludicrous to me. I can't fathom ever letting her go.

"So I'm your prisoner."

"If that's the way you want to take it." I can't go into how I'm fucking obsessed with her. No, I want to work my way into her heart. How the fuck am I going to manage that shit?

She spins around and angrily lets loose her attitude. "What I'd like to do is get the fuck away from all of you. One after the other: abusive, criminal, cruel."

"Baby, stealing you is the only illegal thing I've ever done."

"Don't *baby* me. I'm a married woman. Not some whore." She puffs out her chest, trying to appear tough, but all it does is show her fabulous tits and those stiff nipples that are going to be in my mouth very soon.

"I never said you were a whore, but you will be mine, and you're going to love it. I'm going to make you scream my name, begging for more every single day."

"Bullshit."

"Watch your mouth." She can curse all day long, but I want to see her get smart with me. I have a feeling it's going to be fun.

"Or what?"

My dick's about to burst through my zipper and show her. "You're testing my patience."

"Well, feeling's mutual." *Keep it coming, sweetheart.*

"You know what I'd like to test?" I close the distance and box her in, letting her ass hit the countertop. My hands straddle her while I keep my hips away from her. I don't want her to feel what she's doing to me just yet. I want to watch her come apart.

"What?" She swallows hard, and visions of her down on her knees taking my cock down her throat makes me even harder.

"How wet you are for me."

"I'm not wet," she protests way too loudly.

"No?" I dip my head a little, my lips nearly brushing the side of hers.

"No." Her voice shakes.

"You have a terrible poker face, but that's okay. I'll just see for myself." She doesn't stop me, and I'm not sure if she's too afraid or maybe just a tad bit curious. Either way, I have a point to prove and a need to satisfy. I slide my fingers up her thigh, watching her pupils dilate. Slowly, I inch my hand up, creeping under the soft material, and drag it down. My mouth waters as I stare at her bare mound that glistens for me. My thick, calloused fingers part her seam, pressing gently against her heat. She shivers, but she doesn't take her eyes off me.

"You are a beautiful little liar. Still. I don't like liars. I can't trust someone who lies to me." I pump one finger inside of her, and fucking hell, she's tight. Did he really fuck her or not? Pencil dick bastard. I'm going to hurt her when I do take her cunt.

"Well, I don't like you, so you will have to cope with it."

I shake my head in amusement. I'm an expert at coping. I've had two long years of coping. My thumb rolls over her clit, eliciting a moan from her lips. Step one: get her addicted to my touch. Everything else will hopefully come in time.

"Fine, beautiful. Let me know when you're done coping, and I'll help you out." I pull my fingers out of her slit. She gasps, and I know I won this round. She wanted to come on my fingers so badly.

I step back and walk out of the bathroom with a smile. I can't fucking do her until I know that she's clean and not pregnant. I want to dive into her pussy and breed her myself.

Her voice carries as she curses me out. Good. I wipe

my hands on a dirty shirt and toss it in the laundry before leaving the room again.

The rest of the day passes by quickly as I deal with other issues with my business. Selfishly, I personally brought her dinner up, but I didn't stay to join her. The vision would be too tantalizing. I climb up the stairs to check on Giada. She's lying in bed watching a movie.

"So good to see you," she mutters as if she missed me. I think she just misses human contact that isn't violent.

"Sorry, I had to work. Did you eat your dinner?"

"I did." Her eyes remain on the TV.

"I hope it was good."

She turns her upper body and looks at me with her lips twisted. "It's definitely better than that shit they fed me there, but honestly that's not saying much."

I ignore her bad attitude because I just love that she's talking to me at all after leaving her hanging this morning. "Anything good on?"

"I haven't seen any television in over six months. It's nice to just put on something ridiculous to watch."

I love that bit of honesty. "That I understand more than you know."

"That's right. Two years in prison. I thought they got all the luxuries that most average working people didn't."

I take a seat on the bench and take off my shoes. "They do, for the most part. However, I wanted out, so I traded my time out of my cell for time working on my company from inside prison and finding out who set me up."

"Do you know who did it? Never mind. It's not like you'd tell me."

She's so damn wrong about that. My feelings for her grow every damn hour that passes. "If I knew definitively, I would. I can say that I believe it's someone close to me."

"Rafael?"

I nod, taking off my tie and setting it down on the chair. "Yes, but he couldn't pull it off on his own."

"I can believe it. If it's terribly cruel, then it's up his alley."

"Thank you. How about we get some sleep and then we can talk in the morning?" I finish removing my clothes down to my boxers and tee shirt.

"You're going to sleep with me?" she gasps, and I'm not sure if it's a good gasp or a fearful one, so I take the latter and reassure her.

"Just sleep."

She crosses her arms, pauses, and then asks, "Do you have a girlfriend or a mistress like Rafael?" It's almost as if she's offended that I don't plan on fucking her.

I need to create some emotional distance since we're going to be physically so close. "No. I'm just a man on a mission. Don't try to use sex to get me to let you go. I promise it's not going to work and will piss me off."

"I'm not the one slipping their fingers in places where they don't belong. Excuse me." She hops off the bed and goes to the bathroom.

She closes the door, and then I hear some movement and she comes back. "I have a problem. It's my time of the month."

"Shit. Okay. Give me one minute." I jump out of the bed, slipping my pants back on and rush out of the room with my phone in hand, waking Rita up. When I get to her room, she hands me two square thin little packets for tonight, and she promises to get more in the morning. "Thank you."

I'm up the stairs two steps at a time. "Are these okay? We'll get you some more in the morning."

"Thank you." She goes back in there with a pair of clean underwear from the bag. I'm kind of glad that she has extras. When she comes out about five minutes later, she's a bit unnerved.

"Are you upset?" She bites her lip and avoids eye contact.

"Why would I be?" If anything, I'm doing cartwheels in my head. She's not pregnant, at least that we can tell.

"Because I probably made a mess on the bed."

"Oh, shit. I haven't even looked." My thoughts were all about making her happy and hoping she wasn't in pain, but I hadn't thought of a mess. Frankly, I wouldn't care. I move the covers, but there isn't any blood anywhere, not even on the blanket. "Seems like we dodged that one. Come back to bed."

"Um…Okay." She climbs back in and I wrap her up in my arms.

"Get some sleep, Giada."

"Goodnight, Santino."

"Goodnight," I whisper, brushing my lips on the top of her head.

Chapter Eight

Giada

I wake up with my head on Santino's chest. It's strange sleeping with any man, but it feels so incredible to be wrapped up in his arms. The soft sound of his breathing fascinates me. Could I be falling for him? No, it's probably just the fact that someone is being kind, who also happens to be sexy. It's nothing more than my hormones going wild. Remembering how he reacted to my period reminds me that I need to go change myself.

I cross my fingers, hoping I didn't have any accidents while I slept. I creep out of bed and hurry to the bathroom. Thankfully I didn't ruin another pair of underwear, so once I'm good to go, I step out of the bathroom.

Santino's still sleeping and he looks unbelievably sexy. I can't believe how gorgeous he is. His tee shirt rode up during the night, revealing just the slightest bit of his rock-hard abs. They are lickable, and my mouth waters with the tantalizing idea of thanking him for his kindness. The way

I feel around him is so hard to explain. It's like he's awakened a lustful side, even though I should be running.

The more I want to run away, the more I want him to give chase. After he left me hanging, I nearly died, but I realized that he stopped because he wasn't trying to force me. The idea that sex was more than just a man getting his rocks off wasn't a novel idea. It's just something I haven't experienced. I see something gentle in Santino. That despite everything, I don't believe he'd hurt me, at least not physically.

He's my captor, my abductor, but he's also my hero. Today I would have met the fate Rafael and his father had in store for me. My period came like it always does, and they would have gotten rid of me so Rafael could pick a replacement. I shiver and can't stop thinking about it. Whoever that girl will be, she has my pity.

"Are you okay?" Santino's deep voice breaks through my thoughts. I look up at him, and he's leaning on his elbow, meeting my eyes.

"Yes, sorry. I didn't want to wake you up."

"Shit, your face still looks pretty damn bad." He brushes my hair out of the way, cupping my jaw and turning my head to get a better look at the damage.

I blush from the embarrassment. Even though he knows what happened, it doesn't make it any less uncomfortable. It's nice that I really haven't seen more than two people since I arrived. I can't take all these strangers seeing and judging. "It hurts, but it's getting better. The pain isn't as intense."

"I have medicine in the cabinet. Please take some and try to get some sleep. Our food should be ready in about half an hour."

I walk back into the bathroom and find some Advil. I grab a couple of liquid gel capsules, walk back out to the bedroom, and then pick up a bottle of water to wash the pills down.

Feeling tired, I crawl back in bed and seamlessly, Santino wraps me up in his arms. I'm sure that he just needs the comfort of holding a woman. I'm not sure if he's gotten lucky with any women since he's gotten out, but after two years, I'm betting he's a horny mess. His hard cock digs into my ass, and I don't even try to move.

"Sorry he's not behaving. It's been an awfully long time." My chest clenches at that revelation.

"I'm sorry."

"Don't be. I'm a big boy."

"I can see. Or rather I can feel."

"That's not helping. I'm about to come in my boxers." He chuckles, and the sound rushes through me like a jolt of energy so damn intense that I'm horny as well. I want more of it.

I spin around in his arms and I reach out, rubbing his shaft through the material. I want to please him. "You don't have to do that," he stammers, but he doesn't pull my hand away.

"I want to do it." I stroke him, but it's not enough. I want to see him come because of me. Reaching inside, I pull out his cock. He lowers his boxers just enough to give my hand the room it needs. "Fuck, I'm going to come fast as hell, Giada. God, Giada," he groans as my hand picks up pace. He's so thick and long that I rotate and straddle his thighs. Then using both hands, I work his massive meat. He reaches up and pulls my blouse over my head. His hands go straight to my breasts, squeezing them. I'm moaning and arching into his grasp.

"You're so fucking sexy. I want to come all over and in you." My pussy's throbbing, and I wish I didn't have my period or I'd slide down him and let him show me how sex should be.

He jerks in my hands, squirting jets of cum all over my fingers and his belly. My hands are a sticky mess, but he takes his hands and smears his cum on my stomach and chest. "If I can't breed you, I'm certainly going to mark you."

"Give me your mouth." He slides his hand around my head and drags my body down onto his before kissing me fiercely. "Soon, I'm going to put my baby in here." His hand splays on my belly. Despite everything, I want that. I don't know how we'll even survive when Rafael learns of it, but at the moment I don't care.

A knock at the door interrupts our kissing. "Yes?"

"Breakfast."

"One minute." He lifts me off of him like I weigh nothing and sets me on my feet, and then he stands too. Swatting my ass, he growls, "Get your naked ass in the shower. I'll be there." He slips on some pants and a shirt, opening the door after I dash into the bathroom. A minute later, he sneaks into the bathroom, disrobing as quickly as possible.

"You shouldn't be in here. I'm showering."

"Well, you shouldn't make me come, but it's not going to stop me from helping you get nice and clean."

His mouth goes to my neck. "Santino," I moan. He reaches around, twisting and pulling on my nipples. It shoots straight to my aching pussy. His fingers move, dipping lower. "You shouldn't. I'm…"

"I know, but I don't care." He cups my mound as the shower beats down on my body. His finger slips past my entrance and he strums my pearl, making me cry out. I've never come before. "I want to hear you come. I want you to know what I'm going to give you every chance I can.

Orgasm after orgasm." He pushes in deeper, stretching me, and it hurts but in an incredibly good way. I lean back on his chest and let him work magic on my pussy. "You're going to come for your man, aren't you?"

"Yes, please."

"Tell me you need it, Giada." He growls in my ear and I come apart in his arms, experiencing my first orgasm. My body's shaking hard against his. "God, that's sexy. Next time, I want you facing the mirror so I can watch you as you come for me." He pulls his fingers from me and then we wash up. His dick is hard again, but he keeps it away from me as much as he can. "Now we're even. We have breakfast out there getting cold. And if you learn one thing from Rita, it's that she gets pissy if you don't eat her food when it's ready."

He kisses my cheek and steps out of the shower first, wrapping a towel around his waist. I rinse off and he hands me one. Thankfully, he leaves me so I can pee. After five more minutes, I'm back in the bedroom with a robe around me and a towel in my hair.

We're in the middle of eating breakfast when he says, "The doctor will be here to check on you soon."

"You called a doctor?" Apprehension runs through me because if someone else sees me they might tell Rafael where I am.

"Yes. Well, he was there when I brought you home." That's some relief.

"Oh. Um. Okay." I haven't had a physical since before I married Rafael, and it was to make sure I was truly a virgin. Santino, I'm guessing, wants to make sure I'm clean from STDs. And I can't blame him. Hell, it's something I've worried about since being with Rafael.

"Listen. I have to run some errands. Be good and watch some movies."

Immediately my ire's raised. I thought he'd be different and I'm crestfallen. "Am I ever going to be let out of our room?"

"Yes. Just not yet. I don't know if he thinks I took you. So until I'm sure, you'll have to stay here."

"Do you promise?"

"Would you believe me if I did promise?"

"I'm not sure." I can't determine the change in his expression. It's as if he's almost closed himself off to me, emotionally.

"Then why should I bother even saying it. Excuse me. I have to make some calls." *Did what I say upset him? Does he expect me to believe him? Should I?*

"Have fun," I remark petulantly.

"Hardly." He gives me his own attitude spurs on more sass from me.

I toss my hair over my shoulder as I brush it. Glaring at him, I hiss, "Then don't."

"I like it when you're feisty." He smiles and then leaves. I nearly melt from that look. He's going to turn me into a simpering fool if I'm not careful.

An hour later, Santino comes back into the room with a bag, and he's not alone. A handsome older man enters. "Hello, Giada. You are looking better."

"I'm afraid you have me at a disadvantage."

"I'm Dr. Francisco Reynaldo. Please take a seat over on the bench so I can get a better look at you." I do as he commands while Santino looks on.

The doctor takes my vitals and then brings out a needle and several vials. "Shit."

"What's wrong?"

"I hate needles." Tears well up in my eyes.

Santino comes to my side and holds my hand. "Look at me, okay? I promise that it won't be that bad." I stare into his beautiful honey-colored eyes, and I barely feel the pinch. "It's almost over." Santino's thumb brushes over my cheek, easing the tension.

After everything that I've been through, it's surprising that I'm afraid of needles. "There, Giada. Now, I just have one more thing for you to do." He waves a clear cup with a blue lid. "You don't need to fill it completely."

"But, I have…Well, I have my period."

"That's fine. Start your stream and then catch a small sample."

"Thank you." I stand up and take the cup.

It's awkward, knowing that they both know what I'm doing, but when I come out, Santino's not there. "Sorry, he had a call he had to take. So I have a few personal questions that I need to ask you."

"Go ahead." He reads off a list of medical questions, making notations. When I peek at the file on his tablet, the name for the patient isn't mine, but I'm guessing that's just in case someone starts asking questions.

Santino comes back and walks the doctor out. "I'm going to take a nap," I tell him. Suddenly with the blood taken, I'm extra tired.

Chapter Nine

Santino

"Santino, don't worry. I'll have the results to you by tomorrow under a different name. Nothing I tell you will be shared with anyone you don't want," Francisco says as we walk down the stairs.

"Thanks, Rey," I say, shaking his hand.

"No problem. She's sweet, and I hope that everything comes out well."

"Me too. Me too." After he leaves, I go upstairs to check on Giada. She's sleeping softly, and I'm lost in how beautiful she is. The past two days have been insane. I need Giada more than I ever expected to need anyone before.

I cover her up and head back downstairs to work. It's hard to do, but she needs as much rest as she can get. Once I have the all clear, I doubt I'll give her a good night's sleep again.

Looking at the clock, it's now after four. The day flew by so fast I forgot about lunch. I hope Rita brought something up to Giada. I'm about to summon Rita when my phone rings. I scoop it off my desk and bring it to my ear and say, "Santino Marchetti speaking."

"Brother, it's good to know you're out." I hold back the bile that rises in my throat. "Where's my wife?"

I'd love to slam his head into the ground right now, but I have to keep it together. "Wow. What a fucking greeting! I don't know where your wife is. Why would you think I'd know anyway?"

"Dad told me how you were eye fucking the little whore." Of course he told him. I have a lesson to teach that old bastard soon. You never put your hands on a woman like that—especially my woman.

Ignoring his reference to Giada, I chuckle hard. "Giada's a beautiful woman. It's hard not to stare at young pussy that looked like a little lost puppy ready to suck my dick. Nevertheless, brother, I haven't had pussy in two years. Getting my dick wet sounds fucking great, but I'm not going to get leftovers from you. I don't want a woman no matter how beautiful with someone else's kid or some damn disease. Speaking of diseases…are you still visiting that hooker?"

"What's it to you?" he snarls.

"I'm just saying. Maybe you should ask her. Don't you guys have cameras at the compound? Maybe she's a little jealous."

"We do, but they malfunctioned last night. Besides, she was with me last night."

"Convenient. Look, I'm not in the mood to deal with your problems. I've got enough of my own. I've been

Stolen Wife

dealing with company matters since I visited Mom and Dad. So if you don't have anything nice to motherfucking say, I've gotta go."

"Sorry, Tino. I just figured I'd ask. I can understand you've been through hell. I've got other girls if you're interested." I'm ready to fucking vomit when he makes that suggestion.

"I want a good girl, Rafael," I say.

"Well, then I can get you one of those," he persists. I'm not interested in anything he has to offer.

"I'm keeping my nose clean. So, I'll do it the old-fashioned way, but if I get desperate, I'll give you a call."

"Suit yourself. When are you coming back to visit?" I bet he wants to know for sure.

"I don't know. I'm sure Mom misses me, but like I said, I'm getting my company back and there's so much shit I'm trying to catch up on."

"Let me know when you do, and we can chat it up. Now I need to find that bitch and ring her neck before tossing her around to the crew."

I control the rage in me because it doesn't do me any good to lose it. "Nothing's changed, I see."

"Nope. The dumb bitch is infertile. That pisses me off more than anything. A wasted virgin. I should cap her parents for selling me damaged goods."

I look up and see Giada staring at me with tears streaming down her eyes. Shit, she must have overheard me. "Good luck. I've got to go. My lawyer's on the other line." I hang up and look at Giada. She walks into my office and closes the door.

"You didn't lock the door," she remarks. I left her door unlocked because I hoped that she wouldn't run out.

With Rafael calling, there's no guarantee that one of his men isn't lurking around. I can't have her roaming now.

"I don't want you out of the room. I thought I told you that." I march her ass straight upstairs to our room and slam the door shut. "Keep your ass in there until I'm done. Then we'll talk."

"If you don't want me, then why the fuck am I here?" she shouts through the door. Fuck, I want to go in there and take her right now, but he's onto me. Game changer.

I make a call to my lawyer to act like I really just spoke to him just in case they manage to double check. Our call is short and just as I hang up, my cell phone rings. "Hello?"

"We got people creeping around the house," Joey says.

"Good. Call the cops. I don't want anyone snooping around my property. When you're done, come into my office and report to me." I hang up, seething with rage. What I have to do is going to kill me, but I have to do it.

When Joey comes in, he's brought an officer in with him. "Hello, Mr. Marchetti. I'm Officer Burton. I was informing your man here that I can't arrest the people in the vehicle for loitering, but I warned them to stay away and waited for them to pull off. If they should return, then you can call again and we'll treat it as stalking."

"Who the hell was lurking out there?" I question.

He looks at his notes and then says, "Faustino Milan." One of my father's goons that was at the house the day I was there. This changes everything. I won't be visiting my father's ever again. I can't believe that they were so bold. They must not understand the monster they created.

"Okay. I see." He hands me a copy of the report he filled out for my records.

"Thank you, Officer." I shake his hand and walk him to the door, staying there until he drives away.

"In my office, *now*." My teeth are grinding as I think about the chance that they could have spotted Giada. There's only one vantage point that would allow it, and I'm hoping that they didn't see it.

"Sorry. I tried to get him to leave, but he wanted a word with you before he could file a complaint. Besides, without letting him in, it would look suspicious."

"I'm not pissed. It's smart, but I have an idea. I'm going to need you to visit some family in Ireland."

"I don't have family there," he remarks, looking at me with suspicion.

"You do now." Understanding my meaning, he listens as I continue to explain my plan.

After everything is set up, I say, "I'm going to speak to her."

I stand up and walk out of my office and upstairs. Unlocking the door, I see her sitting on the bed watching television. I lean on the mattress and grab the remote, clicking it off. Closing the distance, I hover over her, grabbing her by the hair and tugging her head back so she can feel how much she drives me nuts. "Now, it's time we talk about that mouth of yours," I say as I skim my lips over her jaw.

"Whatever. Just another Marchetti male." She knows exactly what she's doing.

"Watch what you say. Don't make me do this the hard way, because trust me when I say that's not what you want."

"I knew you were no different. Sold me a lie and then trapped me."

"Oh, you're mistaken, and I thought I made that perfectly clear. I want you here, and I want you in every damn way imaginable, but I'm not going to tell my brother that."

"But I'm everything you said you didn't want."

"Yes, part of that's true."

"Get away from me. I can't, Santino." She pushes my chest, and that's when I see the sparkle on her finger. Snarling like a wild beast, I stare at the rings she has on.

"What the fuck are you wearing?" I grab her fingers and yank the rings off. I want to melt these fuckers down and sell them for scraps.

"Hey! Those are mine," she exclaims.

"The hell they are. You. Are. Mine. Don't wear another man's gift again—especially from *him*."

"You're an asshole."

"Do you really want to go back to him?" I question. She's hurt, so she's trying to retaliate, but that's not going to work.

"No."

"Then don't ever play that fucking game with me again." I wave the rings in front of her face.

"I hate you." She crosses her arms, but I'm betting it's to hide her pebbled nipples. She's turned on, and it's all in her expression.

"Well, that's too fucking bad." I crush my mouth to hers, then pull away quickly. "Goodnight."

I walk out of the bedroom, hoping that the next time I come in there, she's sleeping. I can't have her fight me on this next step. It's going to kill me to let her go, but I'm expecting a raid tomorrow.

Chapter Ten

Giada

I don't know what came over me other than to say I'm fucking losing my mind. I want him, and yet—I shouldn't. I shouldn't have said what I did to Santino, but I did.

The thought of him hating me cuts deep, so much that I blurted out my pain in the form of anger. The way he looked at me with such sadness in his eyes when I said I hated him broke me. I cried for two hours, thinking that I'd gone too far.

Finally calming down, I prepare for bed and watch some television. I'm addicted to *The Office*. By the time I turn it off, it's well past midnight and he's not here in our bedroom where he should be. Two days and I let him into my heart. How could I have been so naïve?

He's just like his brother: cold, cruel—a total bastard, but then why do I want him around?

I lay in bed and sob until I'm too tired to keep my eyes open.

"It's for the best," Santino whispers as his lips kiss my forehead.

"How can it be?" I plead. My heart's breaking in my chest, pain radiating through every inch of my body. He squeezes my ass and then kisses me goodbye.

"You're too much trouble for damaged goods." He shakes his head, staring at me in disgust, and walks away.

"No!" I scream, startling myself awake and into a sitting position.

With a sigh, I wipe the sole tear that slid down my face. I reach out for him, but Santino's not there. Looking around, I'm not in his room anymore. Was the dream real? Shit. The sun's shining through a large window, but I'm not sure where I am.

"Ms. Giada, good morning."

I nearly jump out of my skin when I stare at a large man standing in the doorway. "Oh my goodness. Who are you? Do you work for my…Rafael?" I scooch back on the bed, bringing the covers to my chest.

He rolls his eyes. "No. I don't. I work for Santino."

"Where is he? Where are we?" I ask.

"We are safe away from New York." This is the game he wants to play? I'm going to bombard him with questions until I get the answers I want.

"Where's Santino? I want to talk to him," I demand, trying to gain some backbone.

"Right now isn't the best time."

"I don't understand. Is he busy?"

He shrugs, ever so annoyingly indifferent. "I'm not sure, but he's not here."

I'm here alone with some guy I don't know? Shit. "Oh God, you kidnapped me?" I'm searching the room for something I can bust him over the head with. There are a couple of things, but by the size of this guy, I'm betting it's not going to work.

"No. I didn't kidnap you. I'm here to watch over you. You can roam around the house and the beachfront, but I'm afraid the ocean is off limits."

"I'm confused. Are we like on the Jersey Shore somewhere?"

"No. Things are complicated." He rubs his head. "Just treat this as a getaway. This is a very lovely beach house and the sand looks spectacular. I'll prepare a meal for you. Then I must leave you to it."

I stand up, and I'm dressed in the same clothes I went to bed in. Santino sent me away. Maybe I'd become too much trouble.

"You'll find your closet is full and your necessities can be found in the bathroom." He leaves me standing in the middle of a large bedroom that's almost completely white. The four-poster bed has a gauzy white canopy that gives the room a romantic element. A large television is the centerpiece of a wall full of bookshelves. The room is something I would love to have on any other given day, but without Santino, it feels empty.

I exit the room and find that the rest of the house is as equally beautiful with gray accents to match the almost all white décor.

A cool breeze blows across my arm as the patio doors open and the guy in the suit walks back in. "Sorry, I hope I didn't startle you."

"No, but I don't even know your name," I tell him.

"It's Joey. Santino said that he'll call in a couple of days. For now, please enjoy this place. I'm going to walk the perimeter."

"Why isn't he here?" I have to know why he's not with me.

"He has a company to run."

"Why didn't he just dump me somewhere?" I'm not only pissed, I'm hurt.

"I don't know. Just enjoy. Is that really so damn hard?"

"You're not very nice." I can see I'm working his nerves. Maybe that'll get him to bitch to Santino and then he'll just let me go. Then what am I going to do? It's not like I have anywhere to go, and I sure as hell never want to be anywhere near Rafael again.

He rubs the bridge of his nose, clearly annoyed. "I'm sorry, but I'm not going to give you the answers you're looking for so you might as well stop asking."

"What would be great is my freedom," I remark as I roam around the main living area. It's an incredible beach house. Too bad I'm not interested in being trapped here. A prisoner in paradise.

"Take it up with the boss when you talk to him, okay? Until then, I'm going to do my job."

Flipping him off, I go out to the porch facing the ocean. Leaning up against the railing, I watch the waves crash onto the beach. The water's fairly clear, so I know we have to be somewhere south of New York. I've never traveled, but I've seen the travel brochures for getaways.

I decide to take a walk in the sand. As my feet hit the warm, grainy surface, I feel a hint of sadness. I wish I met someone who cared for me. I wish it were Santino, but that's pointless.

Day two into my new damn prison, and I haven't heard from Santino. I'm starting to think that I'm doomed to be forever locked up. We're in a very isolated location. The cook is in the kitchen, and I'm not allowed to be in there when he's working. Still, I sneak inside there.

"Hello."

"Um…good morning, ma'am."

"So do you need any help with anything?"

"No, thank you."

"Giada," Joey barks at the kitchen door.

"Excuse me. I think I'm in trouble." I wave him off and follow Joey's stalking form. "What's wrong now?"

He grabs my arm and leads me into the little office there. "I told you not to talk to the employees."

"Why not?"

"Because I'm trying to keep you from being discovered. Can't you just act like your life is in danger?"

"Um…what life? I'm just going through the motions."

"Ugh. I'm going to need a raise after this."

"Whatever. I'm going to watch some television. If that's okay, sir," I sneer.

"That's perfectly fine." He leaves and doesn't come back for a long time, so I get curious and look for him. He's on a ladder installing cameras around the perimeter of the beach house. All I have to do is push the ladder from under him and then run, but I don't know if I have it in me. Besides, it's not a big fall and he'll probably catch me before I get far.

I go back to the living room and put on a movie. When he comes back in, he says, "Hey, it's good of you not to knock me down."

"No problem." How did he know I was there?

"Your reflection."

"Damn it, I didn't mean to say that out loud."

"You didn't. I can read it in your eyes."

"Well, next time I'll have to be sneakier."

"You can try." *And I will.*

Chapter Eleven

Santino

It's been a full two days since I drugged Giada and put her on a plane, sending her away from me. The pain in my chest feels like it's getting more intense with every hour that passes.

She probably wants to punch me in the dick for this latest abduction, but it was for the best. She wouldn't go willingly because she doesn't trust me. I felt it after our fight. Seeing her again is all I can think about, but it's not safe for her until I deal with my family and their inquisition.

A friend of mine in law enforcement sent me a text about an hour ago, but I'd already expected the Marchetti family to not let up.

Rita, Jasper, and Martin help me prepare for the visit I know is coming. We clean the house and show no signs of Giada's presence. The gate buzzer rings. I hit the screen on the security system, opening it when I see it's my lawyer.

When he comes in, we shake hands. "It's good to see

you. I'm assuming there's a reason you summoned me so early."

I pat his shoulder and lead him into the living room. "Come on, let's have a seat. Do you need something to drink?"

"Yes, a cup of coffee would be great." Rita goes to make us some coffee while we sit down. "So? What's this about?"

"It seems I'm about to be visited by the sheriff's office with a warrant any minute now."

Tilting his head, he asks, "For what?"

"They're under the impression that I kidnapped Giada Marchetti."

He knits his brows and tilts his head. "Your brother's wife?" I hold back the growl, swallowing back the bile that pools in my throat. The less people know the truth, the less people who have to lie for me. Although, he's a lawyer so he's probably a fucking expert at it.

"That's what they believe." My tone even strikes me as gruff, and he eyes me suspiciously. I can't reveal my secret just yet. I trust Dimitri because he's one of the people instrumental in securing my freedom, so I try to ignore the visible tension running through him.

"Why?" Dimitri stammers on the word, and I can't let go that something's bothering him.

Staring at my friend, I ask, "Are you okay?"

The sound of footsteps stops him from replying. He takes the coffee that Rita brings in, setting it on the table next to him. "Thank you, Rita."

"You're welcome."

She hands me my cup and then excuses herself. "So you were about to say?"

"Yeah, nothing that should worry you. It's just this Russian asshole called me this morning."

Stolen Wife

"I'm sorry. Anything I can do?" Shit. That's probably what's got him shaking. He looks squirrelly today.

"No. It's okay. So, the warrant?"

"Listen, I don't know how they got it, but I'm guessing the judge they got to sign the warrant is in their pocket because they don't have any evidence that I took her."

"Really? I'll do all the talking." As my lawyer, he's not going to let them get away with it.

"Good. I'm not in the mood for this." I drink my coffee with a frown.

"How do you know they're coming?"

"A little birdie told me." Seconds later, the squad cars pull up to my house. "Let the show begin."

I buzz them on through because I'm ready to have them in and out of my house as quickly as possible.

I wait just inside the door for them to come up the steps. A slender man in a cheap suit approaches with six other uniformed officers. "Mr. Santino Marchetti. I'm Detective Romo, and I have a warrant to search your premises for Ms. Giada Marchetti."

"On what grounds?" my attorney asks, stepping in front of me. *Ah, he's back to normal.*

"Who are you?" He narrows his eyes at Dimitri.

"I'm his lawyer, Dimitri Stanislav."

The detective slaps the warrant in his hands. "Read it."

Dimitri does just that before he passes it to me. I skim through it and nearly laugh out loud. "Last known person to see Mrs. Marchetti after making lewd advances to her in front of several witnesses."

"Interesting. That's not good enough. I wonder how much the judge is taking," Dimitri adds.

Detective Romo throws his hands up and shrugs. "That's none of my business. I'm just doing my job."

I nod. "Okay. That's fine. Then once this is over and

you don't locate her? Maybe you should ask them why they think she didn't just run away?"

"What makes you think she did?"

"All I know is the woman I met looked malnourished, scared to meet my eyes, and my father spoke for her. If that doesn't say captive, I don't know what is. Maybe she ran away."

"You think it's a ruse?" he questions, trying to read me.

"I don't know. All I know is that the second she was gone, they were calling me wondering where she was."

"That's good to know. I already read a complaint that one of your father's men had been on your property yesterday."

"Well, I told you they believe I took her just hours after I met her. It makes no sense, but I never pegged my brother to be smart."

Less than five minutes pass when three officers come down the stairs and then two come from the other direction.

The only female in the bunch says, "Sir. We've searched this place from head to toe. There's no sign of her and no female personal effects except for the chef's belongings."

Looking sheepish, the detective says, "Very well. I'm sorry to have bothered you."

"I hope to never see you again. I don't trust any of you."

"I'm not your enemy, Mr. Marchetti." Yeah, at this point, anyone who isn't a trusted friend is my enemy.

"Says the man that searched my house with a flimsy excuse for a warrant."

"It's my job." He tilts his head slightly, bidding goodbye before he walks out the door.

Immediately my staff is gathered in front of me. I type

on my phone and show my staff. ***Run the scanners now.***

Once my office has been cleared of any listening or recording devices, my lawyer and I enter it. "I had to prepare for this moment. They wasted no time. I don't know what they think would happen. Even if she had been here, for all they know she could have ran away from that house. It's legal for her to pick up and leave."

"But…"

"They had her trapped," I say, pouring a glass of scotch and bringing it to my lips. As I do, I get a motherfucking whiff and set it down. A second later, I run to my computer and bring up the security camera footage. Just what I thought. One of the officers searching distracted Martin long enough for another one to put something into the decanter.

I step out of my office and holler to my staff to come downstairs immediately.

I come back inside and Dimitri asks, "And she's not here?"

"No."

"That's all I need to know. As for the other matter, are you ready to head to your office to go over the cameras from the office?" We left enough time to pass to see if any employees snuck into my office, knowing I wouldn't be back until Monday.

"They aren't expecting me until Monday, that's for sure." Dimitri reaches for the glass I set down. "Don't drink that." I take the glass away from him and set it on the sideboard.

My staff walks into my office sans Joey who I sent with Giada as her security although it should be me who's protecting her. "What's going on?" my lawyer asks.

"I called you in here because someone is trying to kill

me." I wave my glass around. "My surveillance cameras point to one of the officers who was in here, but it's also the fucker who came in this room with him. Don't drink anything in this house before checking every single camera."

"Oh my God," Rita exclaims.

"Like I said, check every camera. From the smell, I'm betting the poison is cyanide. I'm going to toss it, but make sure you guys double sanitize everything. Go shopping for new food. Do whatever is needed to make sure this place is safe again. From now on, we won't let anyone in here without triple security measures. I didn't come this far to be taken out by my asshole family and their minions. Dimitri and I are going to be working in here for the next couple of hours."

"Before you get busy working, I found devices in your bedroom," Martin says.

I shake my head, thinking they truly had balls of brass to do that. "I knew they would. I wonder how many of these bastards work for Marchetti. What kind of devices?"

"Both recording and visual."

Smiling, I say, "Very good. Cover the one and move the audio device to the television and put on something loud, preferably porn. Let's give them something to enjoy."

"Sounds like a plan." They leave us and start the cleaning process.

"Let's log into the system from here and run through it. Thankfully, the cameras only record when someone enters the room." We take the seats in front of my desk, turning on my laptop to get things started. Once the application is opened, we press play.

The camera turns on twice during the day where the receptionist drops off documents in my inbox. The next time it turns on, it's about ten and the building should be empty, but it seems someone's interested in my office. I watch as the receptionist comes back in and slips her hand under my desk, pressing something to the underside. We couldn't make it out from that angle, but there's no doubt she put something under there.

"Is there a way to tell what she put in there without going in?" If it's a listening device, that can easily be dealt with, but if it's a mini explosive, that's another matter. I'm going to have my friend meet us at my office with the necessary equipment to scan the room without getting close to my desk.

He shakes his head. "Not that I know of."

"Shit. Maybe we should make a run to the office with Jacobs."

"Okay. That works for me. Let me check the exterior cameras. I'm not feeling very trusting."

"Of course." I pull up the security cameras to see if anyone is lingering or if they were fucking with my cameras. The officers came and went from the house without coming near the vehicles.

"Ready?"

"Yes." Thank fuck they didn't mess with the cars. Maybe it was too obvious that there were cameras or because the buzz of cop cars drew the attention of my neighbors. Either way, we safely drove out to the office.

On the way there, I call in some favors, doubling my security at home and the office. Shit. There's no way I can let her come back into this mess. I want eyes and ears everywhere except our bedroom. There is just too much danger to bring my Giada home, but I miss her so much it's fucking unexplainable. Having been what I have been through, I know life can change in a blink of an eye, but damn, she entered my world and I can't go back to life without her in it, so I might have to speed up my plan for revenge.

My phone rings as soon as we enter the parking garage, sending an ominous feeling into the pit of my stomach. It's a number I don't know, but I refuse to cower, so I answer. "Hello."

"Son, we need to talk." I can't believe he has the nerve to call me at all. Two years in prison, and I only saw him during the sentencing phase of the trial and once when he brought my mother in to see me.

"Son? Since when has that been? I let you play along with that loving father act in front of my mother because I wanted to see her, but at this point we have shit to say to each other. Did you think I'd have the cops tear through my home at your behest and I wasn't going to act like shit happened?"

"It's not like that."

I'm torn between laughing and snapping off. "It's not like that? What kind of bullshit are you on?"

"You're the only one who could have gotten to her." Oh, so he believes it's still me that has her. Well, it's not like they're wrong, but I've left no trace of her being in the house.

"Oh, really, because after two years in prison, I suddenly want to get to a woman I just met and kidnap her. How the fuck was I supposed to get to her?"

"The window to her room or the front door."

"And how am I supposed to get into Rafael's room to steal her?"

"She's in your old bedroom. You would have noticed that when you pulled up yesterday."

"If I'd been looking for that. Now quit fucking harassing me."

"Santino, the guards were in the middle of a break

when it happened, but they also didn't see anything on the cameras either."

"Again. What makes you think I had shit to do with it? I already explained it to Rafael, the cop that came here, and now you. I'm done with you. I have a motherfucking life to lead that doesn't include you."

"What about your mother?"

"I've thought about that for a long time. I love her and always will, but I learned to live without needing her. I'm going to miss her, but since you didn't see fit to let her speak to me when I was locked up, what can I do?"

"I want a meeting."

With a chuckle, I give him a, "Hell, no."

"I'll kill her."

I do my best to control my rage because I know exactly who he's referring to, but I don't want him to know that he can get to me. He spent my entire childhood trying to break me, and I learned to keep him at bay. Now isn't the time to crack. "Who?"

"Your mother."

"You'd kill your wife just because I won't give you a chance to off me again? That's not logical. Still, that's wonderful that you said that because I'm having all my calls monitored at the moment. I hope you enjoy prison. Ha. Damn, it's going to be nice."

"You are bluffing." The fool let me hear the hint of panic in his voice.

"We'll see. Bye." I hang up and look at Dimitri. "Did you get every word?"

"I did. Now, let's make the call." We finally get out of the vehicle and as we start toward the entrance, shots ring out.

"Duck," I shout.

We both fall to the ground and move out of the line of

the shots. Each bullet echoes through the concrete parking garage, ricocheting off the beams. The sound rips through the air, and I'm growing more pissed by the second.

I look over to Dimitri who's against the exterior wall behind a parked SUV. "Are you hit?" I ask as I keep my head down.

"They got me. I'm sorry." I crawl over to him just as the bullets stop.

"Son of a bitch." He's bleeding from the chest, and I'm praying that he pulls through but it looks pretty fucking rough. There's blood everywhere. "Dimitri, talk to me."

"Here's this." He extends his arm a little, showing me his briefcase. "Please pass it along to my family. I'm so damn sorry."

"You have to hang in there." He's struggling to breathe, wheezing with every rise and fall of his chest. He must have been hit in the lungs. Shit. I call 911 and practically shout out the information. "I need an ambulance in the 3rd floor section B of the parking garage at Woodbridge Tower. Someone opened fire on my lawyer and me." I'm shaking as I get the words out.

It feels like forever as I press a shirt from my car to his wound. "Stay with me. Help is on the way." He chokes up blood as I hear the sirens in the distance. I hope they can save him.

Cautiously, I stand and wave the ambulance over to us. Reluctantly, I step aside to allow them to treat Dimitri.

"Santino, whatever happens…you get your woman," Dimitri groans out. He closes his eyes, and I pray it's not the last time. So I'm not as slick as I thought I was. The medics move into action, quickly working on Dimitri.

A notification beeps on my phone. ***Glad you got the message, Mr. Marchetti.***

Who the fuck is this? I type furiously back.

A messenger.

You're a dead man. You fucked up now. I have to contact Dimitri's family. He doesn't have any in the States. The only family is his cousin in Russia. I don't know anything about that, but I'll be calling as soon as I can. I'm sure the answers are in his phone or briefcase.

"Sir, you're bleeding as well."

"It's probably Dimitri's blood," I tell him without taking my eyes off the scene in front of me.

"No, sir. It's dripping down your arm." I look down and see that I have a decent-sized tear in my suit and flesh. It didn't go through the skin.

"He's more important."

"Still, they're loading him. We'll treat you on the way." I jump in the back with both of our briefcases.

I try to avoid listening to them talk as they work on him because I'm not ready to deal with the news that he died. The ride is short, thankfully. They rush him into the emergency room and drag me into a triage area to patch up my wound without the bumpy road.

"Hello, Mr. Marchetti. Let me have you fill this out while we wait for the police to come."

"How's my friend?" I'm not too damn concerned about myself, but it's Dimitri who has me worried.

"He's in surgery. I can't say what's going to happen. Gunshot wounds aren't always as clean as yours."

I wince from the slight pain of the syringe he injected in my arm. "What's that?"

"It's an anesthetic for the stitches."

"Shit, you could have stitched me up without the extra pain," I grumble.

He laughs at me like it's funny. "You say that until I'm halfway done." He doesn't bother to look up at me as he works on my arm. After a minute, he raises his head.

"You're all done. It should heal pretty nicely." I'm surprised that he finished, and I didn't feel a damn thing except the first prick of the needle.

He tosses his gloves out and then washes his hands in the sink. "I've prescribed an antibiotic for you. Take the full dosage even if you feel well." He then goes to the computer and makes notes in my file.

"Why? Is it infected?" I look down at my arm like I'd know the real difference. Frankly, it just looks like a large cut.

"No, but it could be. Trust me; you don't want one to seep in."

"Thanks." He's got a point. I don't want anything, or anyone, in the way when I go to claim Giada.

"Take care, Mr. Marchetti. The nurse will be in here with your discharge papers and prescriptions."

"Thanks again." We shake hands and he leaves the room. I hop off the more comfortable version of a prison mattress and adjust my clothes. Both my shirt and jacket are ruined, so I slip my undershirt back on and toss my dress shirt over my shoulder, giving no fucks if anyone has a problem with it.

Chapter Twelve

Santino

AFTER BEING DISCHARGED, I MEET MARTIN OUT IN THE lobby. He's brought me a new change of clothes. "Thanks," I say as we both walk into the bathroom, so I slip on a clean shirt. When I switch them, Martin steals a look at bandage, examining it.

"Damn, Santino, you're lucky. How's Dimitri?"

Shaking my head, I sigh. "I don't know. Fuck, I have to call his family. Do you have their information or anything?"

"I don't."

"Damn." I slip on the dress shirt and straighten up before we head back to the lobby and take a seat. As they released me, they told me that I might feel weak and I should rest. I didn't believe them until right now.

"I need you to go back to the house and secure it."

He nods and stands. "I will."

"Thank you, my friend." I stand and give him a one-armed hug.

105

"Take it easy. Let me know if you need anything."

For the next three hours, I wait outside the ER for news on Dimitri. Searching through the briefcase he gave me, I see his cousin's number on a paper, so I leave a message for him to call me in the morning. It's only two in the morning there.

I'd just put everything back inside the briefcase when the surgical nurse finally comes out to tell me that he's made it through surgery, but the battle is an uphill one. I call in my team who helped me with Giada and have them bring in their own security for him. One by one, everyone but me leaves. My life feels like it did before, completely out of control.

I've already been questioned by cops and a Detective Morel who's been assigned to Dimitri's case, giving the complete rundown of what happened over the past twenty-four hours. It's already six at night when I see all of them return with the detective who had been at my house this morning.

As soon as he's a foot away, I punch him dead in the face. I'm surrounded by cops who grab my arms behind my back. "You work for my father. You tried to have me killed, you piece of shit, and I have the fucking proof."

"I didn't do shit, but officers, release him. Let him show me the supposed proof," he orders, rubbing his jaw. The cops release me, and I pull up footage from my cameras on my phone. It's been already cued up for this purpose. I play it for them, and they see the cop drop the cyanide tablets into the decanter. "Who the hell is that?" he asks one of the officers who also had been in the house.

I watch their reactions. Either they are incredible liars, or they really have no idea who this guy is. "I don't know, sir. He's not one of our regulars. When he pulled up, he told me he came for backup per the judge."

"What?" both detectives say simultaneously.

"Yeah, and that guy was his partner." He pointed to the one who dropped the cyanide tablets in my decanter. "His car number was 9176. I only remember because it's the opposite of mine, 6719. And I think his name was Vincent." He points to the guy distracting the other guy.

"Do you swear you don't know them?" Detective Morel asks Romo.

"You can check everywhere. I'm on the up and up. I can't stand the Marchetti family, especially Rafael Sr.," Detective Romo says.

"We have something in common," I remark. "If you cross me, I'll suddenly become the killer they accused me of being. I will do whatever I can to come out of this war alive."

"Understood." He chuckles to himself as if he's thinking of something funny. "Now I know why I was put on this one."

"Why?"

"I was married to one of his mistresses five years ago. I hate the prick. He started screwing her to get at me on the force. He wanted me to lose it and get myself fired or dead."

"I'm sorry about her. He's a piece of shit."

"Frankly, I'm hoping his wife got away. From what I learned, she came from the Avanti family and there's rumors that they dabble in the underage human trafficking business. The Feds are handling the matter and don't want us interfering in their sting, so it's only rumors on my end."

"That's my take on it." I'm not going to tell him shit. I still don't trust him at all. "Enough about that. What about my place? The whole place needs a scrub down after your men spent thirty minutes tearing through it."

"Sorry. Take it up with the department with a bill. You obviously aren't going to want us in your home again."

"Damn right, I don't." I don't want a single cop anywhere near my property if I can help it.

"Excuse me. Can I have a word with you, Mr. Marchetti?" Morel interrupts. He grabs me by the bicep and tugs me gently. I follow him to the side away from the rest of the officers. "I'm sorry, but I have some questions about your friend."

"Go ahead and ask."

"Do you have an idea who did this?" Okay. Why couldn't he ask me that in front of the others? It's a simple question unless he truly doesn't trust Romo either.

"I don't know who, but I was more than likely the target." It's an honest answer.

"For a man proven innocent, you're in a lot of trouble lately."

He has no idea what the past few days have brought, much to my chagrin. "Yeah, well. I went away because they wanted me out of the picture."

"You know. You look so damn familiar to me," he says, rubbing his chin.

"Maybe you saw my trial on TV or some shit."

"No. It's not that. I'm thinking of a murder victim." I cock my brow at him. "He worked for your father a long time ago."

"Really?"

"Yes…and he was married to your mother."

"What? What the hell did you just tell me?" I bite out in a hushed whisper.

"Listen. I can't give you more details here."

"Fine. Let's go down to the police station and you can fill me in."

"Sounds good." I walk over to my security, telling one

of them to follow us in my vehicle. I'm not that naïve to trust some random-ass cop especially after the past two years.

I let him take me in his unmarked car and we go to the station.

About halfway there, the silence gets the better of me. "So tell me a little more."

"I'd just joined the police force when the call came and was the first on the scene. I didn't have any experience, and he'd been the first death I'd ever seen. I felt sick to my stomach, so as soon as the detective arrived, I'd been told to move along."

"What did you do after?"

"I took the report and typed it up. They sent me out to canvas the area next day, but with business offices in the vicinity, most people had already gone home before the shooting occurred."

We arrive at the station and I can't help but turn my head in every feasible direction to check for danger. I'd look crazy to anyone else, but Morel is looking around as well. Several officers are staring at us as he leads me to an interrogation room. "Would you like anything to drink?"

"A bottle of water would be good."

"Okay." I wait in the room for about twenty seconds when he hands me a water bottle and then excuses himself. "Give me five minutes to get everything together."

I nod and twist open the cap, guzzling it down in one long drink. I hadn't realized how thirsty I was until I took the first drink. It's been one hell of a day, and I have so many questions floating through my mind.

My mind races while he's gone. I'm anxious for news on Dimitri. I send a text to my guards at the hospital. They reply a minute later. ***No change yet.***

When he comes in, he's holding a new manila folder. "The case is closed, so you can keep this copy."

My hands are shaking as I open it up. The first picture I see is my mother posing with a man who looks just like me. This answers the question of my paternity that I planned to ask my mother about.

"Do you think my mother knew?" She looks so happy in the photo, but she married the guy who might have been the one to kill him.

With a negative shake of his head, he says, "No. See, he was an accountant and got mixed up with your…well, Marchetti's business." I nod as I listen. "You were born a few days before he was gunned down. Your mother was devastated and because of the way it happened, she thought it was Marchetti and told us so, but then it led us to one of the D'Angelo family members, so we prosecuted him. Two years ago, he was shivved in prison."

I'm listening to him, but my brain is trying to comprehend what he's saying, "I don't know what to say."

"I'm sorry, but when I saw you, I knew I had to bring it to your attention that I remembered your father's case. I just didn't realize you didn't know anything about it, including that Marchetti wasn't your biological father."

"You've solved a riddle for me. I've been trying to figure out why they would want to bring me down, and now I know that it has to do with my parentage." I look for his name. *Santino Benedetti.*

"Holy fuck!" My blood boils. I'd been named after a man I knew nothing about. It breaks my heart. There's no way I can let this go, and my mother has a lot to answer for. I slam the folder closed and stand, sending my chair backward, too damn frustrated to sit still.

"This doesn't mean you can go after him."

"Then what the fuck did you give it to me for?"

"Because you deserved to know."

"I need to get out of here." I rub my hand over my face. I'm fucking losing it and I know that the only thing that can make it better is answers and Marchetti's head on a fucking platter. I scoop up the file and walk to the door.

"Wait. I have a bunch of questions about Dimitri." Shit—the whole reason Morel came to the hospital in the first place.

Frustrated, I pull out my cell phone, pull up the text messages, and slide it across the table. "Look at these. I got them seconds after the shooting."

He catches my phone and scrolls through the messages. "Damn it. Wow. Okay. I need a copy of these."

"I'll screenshot them and send it to you." He spits out his cell phone number and I send over the images.

"Do you have anything else besides these?"

"Not about Dimitri, but I recorded a call with my father where he threatened to kill my mother if I didn't take a meeting with him minutes before the bullets started flying."

"Do you have it on you?"

"I do." I play it back and then send the recording to him.

After an hour, he's made some calls and returns with news. "I want you to go home and get some sleep, but I'm planning to call you in ass early. We're going to issue a warrant for the arrest of Marchetti for the threat on you and your mother. I've gone to a judge I know can't be bought." I smile, knowing shit's about to go down.

We shake hands and I follow him out to my security who is waiting for me.

"Let's go home. I want to be back here as soon as we can."

When I get home, I eat something small because I'm

fucking exhausted and just want to sleep, but first I have to call Joey to find out about Giada.

"How's it going there?"

"Things are getting dicey. Your prized cow has been bullish. She's ready to run out of the barn every few minutes." Oh God. Giada would lose her mind if she knew we were referencing her as a cow. It's not cool, but I have no choice. I wanted to keep them off her scent as long as possible, and just in case someone was listening in, I didn't want them to figure out it was her.

"Well, soon she'll settle down. When the calves come. How is your family?"

"They're not much better than the cow."

"Sorry to hear that." I inform him of what happened to Dimitri before calling it a night. Tomorrow, I'll tap into his security cameras and see my woman. It's all I can do at the moment. Soon, I'll be claiming her for sure.

Chapter Thirteen

Santino

As he left to handle the arrest, he adds, "Your brother is going to be brought in for questioning as well."

I've been waiting in the room for two hours when Morel comes back in. "We're separating them right now. We'll bring in Mrs. Marchetti and then you can speak to her." My anxiety kicks in and I'm out of my seat, ready to get this all over with.

I tap my fingers on the file that holds secrets, lies, and a man taken too soon. The door opens, and my mother smiles widely. "Santino, my baby." She throws her arms around me, but this time I don't hug her.

"Mother." She backs off, tilting her head in curiosity. I feel like a bastard for hurting her, but I've been through hell and my life has been nothing but one fucking lie after another.

"What's wrong, mio figlio?"

"What's wrong is that for thirty years, I believed that

bastard you're married to was my father, but you hid him from me." I open the file to their picture and lift it so she can see.

Immediately she breaks down in tears, collapsing onto the chair. Taking the photo from me, she says, "God, I still miss him so much." Her voice cracks and I finally notice the frailty of my mother. She brushes her hand over his face as tears continue to fall. She closes her eyes, bringing the picture to her chest, cradling it. "He'll kill me now for sure now that you know."

"Who are you talking about? Your husband?"

It takes her a few minutes to calm down enough to speak. She looks around the room and sees the camera. "I don't know who's watching, but it's best I tell you the truth either way." She takes a deep breath, trying to calm herself. "Thirty-three years ago, I met your real father in Sicily where I grew up. He was handsome, just like you, although he was shy and well, we fell in love. He was only there for a business trip and had never been there before. It was wonderful. He asked for my hand and my father agreed. We were poor, and he saw the promise in your father's eyes when he said he'd take care of me. We were married about two months later and then I came back to America with him." She breaks down again, sobbing into her handkerchief.

"I loved him so much. It took a while for us to get pregnant with you, but we felt so blessed. Then one day, a new client came into your father's office and wanted his services. Even though your father turned him down, he wouldn't take no for an answer. Your father was beaten badly and had gone along to protect me and our unborn baby. He couldn't wait to see your face. He loved you so much, but we didn't realize that I had captured the eye of the up-and-coming boss of the family, Rafael. At the time, his father had run the operation. When he saw me, he made passes at me, but I refused him always. I'd never betray your father. Things were quiet until two days after you were born. Your father had to finally go to the office and handle some things, but he never made it home. He was gunned down right there."

"And you still married that bastard."

"I didn't know it was him, but I had my suspicions. Then they pinned it on the D'Angelo family almost immediately. The arrest was made that night. I cried for days on end, so much so I was sent to the hospital. When they were to release me, I learned that the state had taken you away from me. I had to find a way to get you back, but it wasn't that easy. By losing my mind over your father, they believed I was an unfit mother. That's when Rafael made me a deal. If I'd marry him, he'd get you back for me."

"I didn't want to, but they already had you living with another family. I needed my sweet boy, so I agreed. The day of the wedding, the papers were signed to bring you back home. It took a few weeks, but you were mine. I got to hold you and love you every day."

"Did you know it was him who killed my father?"

"It was the day your brother was born. We had been fighting like crazy because I was still in love with the ghost of your father. I'd been ready to leave with the both of you boys, but he beat me so badly and I went into labor early." I slam my hand down on the metal table. She pats my hand. "Calm down, Santino. I can stop if you want."

"No, please continue." I'm already picturing what I want to do to that son of a bitch.

"Rafael didn't take me to the hospital right away, though, because he wanted to make sure none of the bruises were visible. I only had a red mark on my face that cleared up before he allowed me to go. Your brother almost died, and he blamed me for it. Then after they put him in the NICU, he came up to me and said, 'If my son dies, I'll kill your little bastard like I killed Benedetti.' He laughed and said, 'God, I looked him right in the eyes and told him that I was going to enjoy his wife and I sure have.' I suffered in the hospital for three more days, hemorrhaging. The only thing that kept me alive was the fear that he'd harm you because God knows how much I ached to go to your father."

I can't even explain how angry and sad that makes me. Fuck, I'd never hurt a woman, especially a pregnant woman. "Is that why you stayed with him all these years?"

"Yes. When you were leaving to start your own life outside of his organization, I told him that I was going with you. That nothing could stop me. The next day he had you arrested for murder. I'm so sorry. This is all my fault. Everything wrong in your life is because of me. Your father's death was because of me."

He trapped her like an animal, using me as the bargaining chip. I can't stop myself. I pull my mom into my arms. "No. It was because of him. If you never married him, I'm sure he would have forced you. He just tried to butter you up. In all these years, he's loved the control he's had over you. I never wondered why you stayed. I knew you feared him. I just didn't know it was because of me."

She pulls back and caresses my cheek. "When I saw Giada, I just knew she needed to get out of there."

I cut her off with another hug because I can't let on that I have her, at least not with ears everywhere. "You're coming with me."

She pulls away and stands. "He'll kill you." She's petrified of him, but I'll never let him touch her again.

"He's already tried several times. Rafael and his father think I took Giada." I made sure I said that loud enough for the camera because I want them to believe that I don't have her. Someone on their team must be watching, but my guys are also watching, and my phone has been recording it all.

I pull back and say, "He's been arrested, and we're going."

I grab her hand and the file and head to the door. My gun is under my coat, and I'm ready to use it at a moment's notice. Morel opens the door and says, "We're going to drop you off under a police escort. He's locked up, and Rafael is in questioning right now."

"Good, but they have eyes everywhere."

"Speaking of, we picked up that officer. One was an actual officer out of the 9th district who is being questioned as well and the other was his thug cousin who works for the D'Angelo family."

"The D'Angelo family?" *What the fuck do they have to do with it? Could they be looking for revenge over one of their own taking the blame for my father's death?*

"Yes. I'm not sure what's going on, but I'm guessing this is more tangled up than I believed."

I arrive at the house with Martin meeting us. "Sir, the house has been cleaned, swept for bugs again, and any food items they were near have been tossed just for safety precautions."

"Good. Now, please prepare a room for my mother. She's going to need a guard with her all the time."

"Get some rest. I'll speak to you in a little while." She nods.

"Can I have this?" She's holding his picture.

"Of course."

"It's been so long."

"This is Andrea and Matteo. They are best to look after your mother." I nod and shake their hands. "Please make sure nothing happens to her."

"Understood."

"Excuse me, but she looks like she's going to crumble. Maybe you should bring her some food and drinks."

"Thanks, Andrea."

"Martin, please have Rita prepare something light."

"She's already getting started. She had to sanitize her entire kitchen. She's been freaking out, and Jasper went to get her all the groceries she needed to calm her down."

It's the first time I can truly smile. "That sounds like her. Thanks, Martin."

"Please excuse me." I go into my office, needing to breathe. My thoughts go to Giada, and it strikes me how I'm doing the same thing. I intend on killing my brother and taking his wife. "Fuck," I grumble.

I read through the documents to see if there's anything that can lead to my stepfather as the killer. I'm going to kill him.

My phone rings, and it's Rafael. I smirk, knowing this was coming. "You better bring back my mother."

"She's my mother too. You know you don't have a monopoly on her. In fact, you had her for two years."

"Dad's going to kill you, and I'm going to watch."

"He's not my dad, but I wouldn't bet on it. I'm going to see you go down, Rafael. You don't deserve the air you breathe. I wonder if Mom will really mind if I strangle you to death myself."

"Please. You're a big puss bag, and don't call my mother a whore again."

"I didn't call my mother that."

"You just said he wasn't your dad."

"He wasn't. Your father killed my dad to steal my mom. You need to ask his ass about that, but he has a death wish I'd love to grant." I hang up on him because he can go to hell. We have nothing to say to each other. War is war.

Chapter Fourteen

Santino

I do my best to sleep, but I'm still trying to get a handle on everything that I learned. My heart hurts for the man I never met and the life we missed together. Then I think about my mother. Would that be Giada? Would she mourn me? Probably not, but damn, I miss her so much. I can't stop thinking about her.

My cell phone rings as soon as the sun is up, and I wonder if my brother wants to threaten me again. I scoop it off the nightstand and see it's a private number. "Hello," I answer, remaining guarded.

"Hello, this is Alexei Bykov. I received a call from Mr. Santino." I hadn't given my last name because I didn't want to use Marchetti, and I didn't have my real last name at the time I called.

"Yes, sir. That's me. Unfortunately, I have some bad news." I pull off the covers and get up. I'm not going to be able to sleep anyway.

"They got him, didn't they?" He sighs.

"Yes. I'm sorry, Dimitri is intensive care at the moment in a medically induced coma."

"Please inform me where to come, and I shall be there tomorrow. I cannot believe he got involved in my business issues. I must go." He ends the call, and I can tell that he's pissed, and he should be. Dimitri was my friend.

As I get dressed for the day, I call the hospital, but the result is the same. It's not looking good, but I hope he pulls through.

A knock on my door disrupts my thoughts. "Come in."

Mom walks over to my bed and sits on the edge.

"Good morning, Mother. Are you feeling better?"

Her eyes are swollen from the tears she shed last night. "Yes and no. I'm glad that you know the truth no matter how painful it is, but the memories of the loss. It feels so fresh all over again."

"Tell me about him, please."

"You are his spitting image, but that I'm sure you're aware of. You also have so many of his good qualities. Your sweetness in all this adversity has shone through and not just with this, but well before you ever went to prison. You thought past the violence and murder to become a better man."

I can't think past it now. "Are you trying to talk me out of killing your son?"

"No. I can't ask that of you and as much as I don't wish it, I don't know if he'll leave you alone unless you do." A part of her will always love her son, but she knows the monster he is.

"Has Junior ever hit you?"

"Almost. What he saw at his father's hands made him believe it was okay, but for all his faults, and there are oceans full, Rafael told him that I was never to be touched."

"It's strange that he would do this because he loved you and then do everything to hurt you."

"That's because he doesn't love me. I'm a possession. At first I was a challenge, then I became an obsession, then his property to guard. He could misuse me, but no one else could."

"I don't get it."

"That's because you have a good heart. You are repulsed by the evil and yet they continue to drag you back into the fray. My sweet boy, I'm hungry and you look exhausted. Let's eat and you can tell me about Giada. Can you walk me downstairs?"

"Of course, but there's nothing to tell."

"You can lie to others, but you cannot lie to me. From the second you saw her, you had that look your father used to give me all the time. From the first moment we met, I knew he loved me. She needs a man like you to make things right."

"Mother, then I will be no better than Signor Marchetti."

"You are a million times better. And she looked at you with loving eyes as well, my boy. Something I never did with my captor."

"I don't know." I want her to look past it all and see me for the man I am. Frankly, I'm not sure she's going to speak to me again after dumping her on a beach. Locked away. Caged again.

"You're lying to yourself." She kisses my cheek and stands. "Let's go. I'm sure I can make something special for you. I've deeply missed you, Santino."

I watch my mother make me breakfast, seeing a new light in her eyes. Rita comes in and smiles. "You two are up early. Do you need my help?"

"Coffee, please," I say.

"Coming right up." Rita needs to feel useful after all this time. I love having her here to care for my mother and soon to keep Giada from working too hard while she's pregnant with our babies.

After breakfast, I excuse myself because there's a lot to do before I head into work tomorrow. The bell to my gate rings just before noon. I check my cameras and almost laugh at the absurdity of the murderous bastard standing at the gate with my brother. "Can I help you?"

"Bring my wife out here," he demands, making me laugh.

"Ha. No. Go away before I have you arrested for trespassing."

"I will get her," he persists, as if that's going to work with me.

"Actually, you need to stay away from her. After all, that recording did say you planned to kill her. There's a restraining order on you. I know that means bullshit to you, but I'm prepared to deal with you should you try." My guards not only surround my home, they are armed. It's one luxury of being well off and with known threats.

"I see. This isn't over. You know, I should have drowned your ass as a baby."

"Well, your fault you didn't. On another note, before you go...does my brother there know that his mistress had your kid and not his?"

"What kind of lies is your mother spouting?" He's turning red, getting heated as he realizes I had something else on him. I'm guessing Junior had no idea about it.

"You think she had to tell me? I never understood why you never let him marry her even though she had your grandkid. Then I did a little digging. You know that DNA test makes you the father and him the brother of little

Antonio. Brother, I'm betting he told you it was a mix up, or did you know you were fucking your father's leftovers?"

"What the fuck?" Rafael Jr. exclaims, staring at his dad with contempt.

"He's lying." He tries to go into an explanation or maybe an excuse, but I don't have the time or patience for it, so I interrupt them.

"Have a good day, gentlemen. Oh, and Rafael—if you need a copy, it was with my attorney's things yesterday before he was shot. I have a copy." They storm off, and I'm betting young Rafe is thinking about it.

The buzzer goes off again and I'm about to bark out that I've called the cops, but the giant man in the camera tells me it's not him. He has four other men surrounding him. "Can I help you?"

"I am Alexei Bykov."

"Please go through my security and then come in." I get up and walk to the foyer. It takes a minute before they're searched. After they leave their obviously illegal guns outside, I invite them in. "Sorry about that, but I've had a rough time lately. I'm Santino Benedetti."

"I thought it was Marchetti." He gives me a suspicious look since he probably looked me up.

I want him at ease. I'm dealing with extra trouble I don't need. "I've just been made aware of my parentage. Please follow me into the living room." I escort them in there.

"Martin, please prepare some drinks for these men."

"Mr. Benedetti, is it?"

"Yes."

"I'm here about my cousin. I don't know who did this exactly, but in Russia the number of people could be staggering."

"I'm not sure if I was the reason for your cousin being targeted. I don't know if you saw those bastards out there."

"I did. Is that what America's Mob looks like, because it is weak."

"Oh no, don't underestimate that piece of shit. The older one. He's going to be my first kill."

"Ha. Mr.—"

"Santino."

"Santino, I can tell you are not meant for this. From the records I pulled, you have a clean nose except for the wrongful conviction. Unless you have sneaky lawyers?" He winks, knowing Dimitri was mine.

"No. I was set up. I'm not in that line of work. Dimitri did his best and worked with my people to get my freedom. I owed him so much, but I might have put him in the way. I'm sorry."

"Do you have any evidence of that?"

"I received this text right after the shooting." I pull my phone out of my pants pocket and bring up the messages.

He reads it and then passes it to the other guys. "I'm not sure it was my enemies, but whoever they are, they are my enemies now."

"Oh goodness." We all turn to see my mother standing there. "I thought you let those other two in." She has her hand pressed to her chest.

I walk to her, giving her a quick, reassuring hug. "Never, Mother. They'll take you over my dead body."

"So who are they?" She crosses her arms.

"Unfortunately, the reason I was at the police station was because my lawyer was shot. His family arrived from Russia."

She clasps her hands to her mouth. "Really? Oh my goodness. I'm terribly sorry. Is he alive?"

"Thank you," Bykov says with a nod. "I hope he survives."

"When can we prepare to see him? We wish to take him back home as soon as he's recovered."

"It's something you have to speak to the police about. They will need a bunch of shit from you before he will be released if he pulls through."

"Very well. Can you give me the information for the hospital? I'd love to check on him."

"Sure. I need to see Dimitri soon, but I don't want to be the reason they make a second attempt." I text it to him. "They won't." He stands up and says, "We will be staying at the Plaza. Can you inform the authorities to contact me?"

He takes his leave with the rest of his men. "That man looks like he's about your age. I'm sorry about your lawyer."

"Me too. Come, let's eat some lunch and then relax for a bit."

Chapter Fifteen

Giada

A WEEK. I HAVE BEEN ON THIS ISLAND FOR A WEEK. Not once have I gotten to hear from or see Santino. He hasn't called, messaged, or visited me. I'm beginning to honestly believe that he's moved on to a new flavor. After all, it's been two years of no pussy. That's got to drive a man like him insane. He's hot, young, and virile. Gosh, remembering the things he did to me reminds me how much he needs to get laid.

"Lunch is ready," Joey says, interrupting my memory of Santino's fingers teasing my pussy to an incredible orgasm.

"Okay." I follow him into the kitchen where the temporary chef has prepared a delicious pasta in a light sauce.

"Thank you." He leaves us to enjoy the meal. This is the only meal Joey eats with me. I like the guy, even though he hardly says a word. He's the only reason I don't jump into the ocean and end it all. Every once in a while, he lets it slip that he's spoken to Santino. He tells me that Santino misses me but refuses to give me the phone. I can't tell if he's telling me the truth or trying to keep me compliant.

"So when can I leave?" I ask after I plop down on the stool.

His expression changes and he tilts his head. "Are you going to ask every single day?"

I roll my eyes and then pop a grape in my mouth. "Yep. I mean, I'm not doing shit here."

He shakes his head and cuts a piece of chicken. "I never met someone who didn't like living in a paradise," he says before taking a bite.

"What's the point of paradise if there's no one to share it with?"

"Damn, what am I? Chopped liver?" He presses his hand to his chest in mock outrage.

"At this point, yeah." I smirk with my head bent toward my plate.

He just scoffs and takes another bite. "Well, tough. I can't let you go anywhere."

"I'm not going to take this shit much more."

"Just give him time."

"I gave him a week already. I hate this. It's worse than being stuck with Rafael."

"Behave."

I know that's crossing the line because nothing is worse and then again, to me it's painful to think of Santino and to know he's abandoned me. "Whatever. I'm not going to sit around like a puppy dog. I'm going into town today."

"No, you're not."

"We'll see about that." I empty my plate into the garbage and then wash my plate. He finishes his and then hands it to me for me to wash. We've set up this routine that works nicely, but even as I set the plate in the rack, I'm thinking about Santino and my mood darkens.

"If you want to go in the water, today's a good day, but I'll be watching you."

"Damn you need to get a girl. Spending your day ogling me is getting out of control," I tease. Honestly, the man ignores me like I have the plague.

"Don't let Santino hear that, or he'll kill me for nothing."

"Whatever. I'm going to change." I head into my bedroom and scoop up my latest read. It's a great book and I'm looking forward to learning what causes them to separate and if they'll get their happily ever after almost all us girls dream of. Since Santino took me, I've dreamt of a life without Rafael and it sends me into a much better mood, but I also picture Santino as my happily ever after.

Slipping out of the house, I walk along the beach for hours, thinking about life. What can I do about it? I know that just escaping Rafael is a blessing, but can I be greedy and ask for more?

"Giada, where are you going?" I stare up at the sky, wishing I can punch Joey in the face.

"I'm not going anywhere. Gosh, didn't you say I could walk along the beach?" I remind him.

"Yes, but you're way past the house." I turn around and look. I can't even see the house anymore.

"Oh goodness. I was lost in my thoughts."

"Let's get back to the house."

"Ugh. Okay." I nod and follow in step alongside him.

"Don't look so down. Things will get better."

"Is he seeing someone else?" It bothers me more than it should. He doesn't owe me anything including his fidelity. I'm not his wife. Hell, I'm married to someone else, but that doesn't stop the pain in my chest thinking of him with another woman after the stolen moments with him.

Joey sighs and then says, "No. Be patient."

"You don't even know what it's like to be caged."

"I do. I met Santino in prison." I wasn't aware of that. Wow.

Surprisingly, I'm not afraid of him after that revelation. "I'm sorry. It's just I felt the taste of freedom and had it taken away." Joey has been kind to me, but I'm lonelier than I've ever been and Santino's the reason for it.

"You need to just remember that things will get better." He's right. They've already drastically improved.

Once we're inside the house, I excuse myself to go lie down. It's not like he spends more than a handful of minutes with me at any given time.

I wake up to the sound of movement in my room. "Who's there?"

"It's me, Santino."

"It's about time." He sweeps me into his arms and crushes his lips to mine. It feels so incredible, and then he's gone.

I sit up in bed, realizing that it was all a dream. Uncontrollably, tears stream down my face. The sound of the phone ringing causes a break in the waterworks. It's still light outside. I must have taken a quick nap.

Climbing out of bed, I walk out into the hallway and there's Joey on the phone.

"Yeah, the cow is getting restless." *Did he just call me a cow?* I can't hear what Santino's saying to him, but he just referred to me as a cow. I glance down at myself. Yes, I put on a little weight, but I was underweight before we came here, so I'm actually healthy looking.

"Okay. I'll handle it, boss." *What's he going to handle? Are they going to get rid of me?* No. I can't see them doing that.

Either way, it appears that Santino wants nothing to do with me and is leaving me to the whims of his henchman.

There's nothing left for me to do but find a way for me to escape. I wait until he goes to his room and then I sneak back into my room and get my things together in a tiny travel bag that's stored in the closet. The best I can do is sleep on the beach while trying to find a job somewhere on the island. I have to play the rest of the day cool.

After I've gotten my gear together, I go into the living room area where Joey's watching television. "Did you have a good nap?" he asks without turning around.

"It was fine. Is there anything made for dinner?"

"Yes, it's in the oven."

Just like that, the timer goes off. "I'll get it." I'm only going to do it so I can steal some snacks for my plan. I take out the baked spaghetti and set up the plates. I take a kitchen towel and wrap up some apples, granola bars and a couple bottles of water and scurry into my bedroom.

When I come back, Joey's in the kitchen. "Where did you go?"

"When you got to go, you got to go," I lie, and he doesn't question it.

He blushes slightly and serves our food before taking his into the living room. It's what he always does, which I'm grateful for especially after his cow comment. In fact, I don't think I can eat a thing. I leave it on the plate and steal a few more pieces of food that travels well and go into my room, locking the door.

At three in the morning, the sounds of the ocean are a little louder tonight. Maybe it's because I feel so damn alone. I slip out of my room and into the hallway with my bag. The house is super quiet. The front door easily opens, and I step out unnoticed. Shit, I should have stolen his car keys. Spinning around, I move to go back inside, but the door locks and I'm stuck outside. Fine. Walking is how it's going to be. Hell, it's not like I know how to drive anyway.

Immediately, I regret what I'm doing because I didn't really think this out. A broken heart can do that to a girl. The moon is full, which probably explains the steady waves crashing against the shore harder than usual. Joey told me that there's hardly ever severe weather here and that we're all clear for at least a week. It gives me a bit of peace to know I'm not fleeing during a tsunami or something.

I'm just about around the beach house, but I'm not sure which way to go. It's too late because I feel arms wrapped around me before I can move. "Where the hell do you think you're going?" I gasp, knowing that it's Santino's voice.

Another dream. I pinch myself. "Ouch."

"It's not a dream, baby. I'm here for you," he growls against the shell of my ear. "Now, why the fuck are you trying to leave?"

"It's been over a week. What the fuck did you think I'd do?" I try to fight him off, but a big part of me loves the feel of his strength wrapped around me. "Get the hell away from me."

"What did I tell you about that mouth of yours? You're going to pay for that."

"Leave me alone. You're an asshole. I hate you." I shove off and start to make a run for it, but he's way too fast for me and I have nowhere to go, and honestly, nowhere I'd rather be. It feels too good to be true, and I hate him for making me feel that way.

He flips me over his shoulder like I weigh nothing and swats my ass. "Time to pay up, wife." How dare he call me that?

"I'm not your wife. Put me down." I wiggle in his arms, fighting him with every step.

"Fine. You want to do this the hard way—cuffs it is." I hear the dangling of the metal and feel my pussy gush just a little. I hate my treacherous body.

Trying to at least put up a fight, I ask him, "Why are you here? Did you come to get your cow?"

"Ha. Is this what this is about?" He opens the door and steps inside with Joey looking on. "Collect her bag and bring it back. After that, head into town for some breakfast and then bring some back for us in a few hours. Thanks."

"Sending him away? About time." I glare at Joey from my upside down position, flipping him off. Joey leaves with a smirk on his fat face.

"That's not nice," Santino scolds me, spanking my ass again. I try not to enjoy it because he's a stupid bastard who trapped me.

"You're not nice." I spank his ass and feel how firm it is, clenching my thighs together to control the lust that I shouldn't feel for him.

"No, I'm not." Santino tosses me onto the bed, kicks off his shoes, and then crawls over me, pinning my arms over my head.

"I don't want you," I spit out, narrowing my eyes at him. His hips dig into mine and his thick cock grinds on my pussy, causing me to roll my pussy up against him.

"What did I tell you about lying to me?"

"I don't care if you don't like it."

"I find it sexy when you fight the need you feel for me. Baby, you're so damn hot that I want to be buried deep inside of you all the time."

"Yeah, you have a funny way of showing it." I nudge my knee into his side, but it does nothing. "Get off of me."

"I'm not going to fuck you until you're ready." He grinds his hips on my pussy one more time before pushing off of me.

"What the hell?" I don't even know how to process his retreat.

"What? I'm giving you what you want."

"Oh, my freedom? Yes!" I jump off the bed and move to the open bedroom door. I turn back around when I don't hear him. Santino doesn't give chase. Instead, he sits on the bed and spins the cuffs with his finger.

"If that's what you believe. I know that's not exactly what you want."

"Really? Then what do I want?"

"You want to be thoroughly well fucked until you've passed out from several orgasms."

"I doubt you could deliver anyway. It's in the genetics." He's on me in a second. He's so fast that I almost don't see him coming. The next thing I know his mouth on mine, giving me a soul-stealing kiss.

"You know I can make you come. We both know it, and I know if I test your sweet pussy, it's going to be dripping with need, isn't it?"

"So?"

"So why waste time fighting when I can show you how much I want to worship your body over and over again." I hear the cuffs close around my wrists.

I pull my lips away from him and use my chest to push back, but he grips me around the waist and holds me tight. "Bastard. Uncuff me."

Stolen Wife

"Not until you tell me the truth."

"The truth?" His hands snake down my sides, sending a shiver through me. I try to hold back a moan that aches.

"Yes, the truth, Giada. Do you want me to make you come?"

"No…" I close my eyes and absorb his touch while lying. A part of me doesn't want to give him the satisfaction of knowing what he's doing to me. Another wants to share everything with him.

This is the first time I get to really look at him in over a week, and he's hungry. His eyes roam up and down my body. "I've missed you, Giada. I know you don't believe me."

"I hate you." I fight back the tears, but the fight is gone in me. I want to be in his arms.

"No, you don't. That's why you're upset."

"You think you know everything, don't you?"

He grabs my bottom lip and tugs gently. "Not at all, but I do know you deserve someone better than me. I just can't let you go." I gasp as his other hand slides between my legs and his lips meet mine again. "Do you want to come for me?"

"Yes, Santino," I whimper, clenching my thighs around his hand.

"Good girl." He chuckles lightly, pulling away from me. I feel the loss and am ready to fight when he turns me around and undoes the cuffs. "I promised if you were honest with me, I'd take them off." He trails the cuffs over my skin, sliding my top up with the press of the metal. Beads of sweat form over my body. I'm not sure if it's from the heat or the way he sets my soul ablaze.

Scooping me up in his arms, Santino carries me back to bed, laying me down and letting his hands linger over my waist. His teeth dig into his bottom lip as he stares at my abs.

He grips and caresses my breasts, plucking on my hardened peaks through the lacy material. Growling, he reaches around and undoes the snap, tugging it off of me. "So fucking beautiful." He bends down and sucks on my nipple before moving to the other one and showing it attention. "You're mine, Giada. You belong to me and always will. Do you need me to prove it to you?"

I shake my head. "I'm not yours," I pant, lying through my teeth. He smiles at me, causing my core to tighten and my slit to drench my panties.

"I told you about lying to me." He reaches up and cuffs my wrists again, but this time I don't even attempt to put up a fight. Smiling, he steals another kiss. "I know you're mad, but I'm going to make it up to you—over and over again."

His tongue dips out, swiping just above the fabric and licking the top of my breast before kissing it. Slowly, he takes his time as he moves his mouth up my body to claim my lips. His fingers slide down my sides, over my hips and onto my thighs. He roughly pulls my leg over his hip, letting me feel his need.

"I'm doing my best to stay in control, but just touching you, tasting you is sending me over the edge." He reaches between us and slips his hand under my shorts.

"I need you, Santino. Take me, please." He stands back up, stripping completely naked. Then his hands come to my waistband, dragging my shorts and panties down together and tossing them somewhere behind him.

"I'm going in bare. I'm clean and you're clean. I need to feel all of you," he grunts, getting onto his knees between my legs.

"Thank God."

"Amen." He lowers his head and kisses me as he lines his cock up with my pussy. I'm turned on and scared at the same time. The tip pushes inside, and I feel completely stretched out. *Holy shit.*

"Santino," I cry out, digging my nails into his biceps.

"Giada, relax. I'm going to make you come, and then I'm going to do it again." Santino presses his lips to my pulse, sucking on my skin, surely leaving his mark. "Mine," he whispers, staring at his handiwork.

Lazily he pushes deeper in me, claiming my pussy as his.

Chapter Sixteen

Santino

HER PUSSY IS SO TIGHT THAT I HAVE TO GO SLOW OR I'LL hurt her. As much as I want to ride her like a fucking bronco, I have to take it easy until she lets me have it all. The feel of her cunt wrapped about my cock is insanely too intense that I feel the pull to come. I can't do that to her. Slipping out of her warmth, I move down between her legs, putting them over my shoulder as I take my first taste of her sweetness. I knew I'd be addicted, and that I am. I lick her from her slit to her ass, nipping her ass cheek before diving my tongue deep in her wetness, stealing every drop of need from her body.

Giada lowers her cuffed wrists and runs her fingers through my hair. I could die a happy man between her legs. Plunging two fingers in, I try to open her up, stretching her wide while sucking on her little nub. "Santino. Shit, oh hell. I'm coming." She thrusts her hips up, grinding her cunt on my face. I eat her up like the best fucking last meal, leaving nothing left on the plate. Rising up, I skim my tip up and down through her slit, stroking her with the underside of my cock until she's whimpering for more.

"Santino, I need you." The way she says my name shoots straight through me and I can't get enough.

"Just what I needed to hear." I push my way back into her heat, doing my best to keep from coming. I take her arms over her head and hold them down as I rock my hips in long, deep strokes. I shudder as I pull out and push back in.

"Fuck me, Santino."

"I'm too damn close, Giada." She ignores my revelation, wrapping her legs around my waist, locking her feet together against my ass, forcing me deeper into her tiny womb.

"So am I," she cries out. I have to taste her mouth. My tongue runs along the seam of her lips until she opens up, letting it slip inside. She moans and comes again. Her pussy seizes up, squeezing my cock until I lose all control, picking up speed until I roar out my own release. I kiss her face repeatedly as I attempt to get my breathing back to normal.

"Giada. Giada. Giada." I love her, but I'm not sure she'd believe me if I said it, so I sigh and then get up. We groan when I pull out. I could stay in her all day, but I want the cuffs off of her.

"Are you okay?" she asks me.

"You're asking me if I'm okay? I'm more than okay, baby." I bend down and scoop the key out of my pocket and climb back on bed and sit up while I grab her arms. "Let me get these off of you."

"Is it terrible that I like them, given everything I've been through?" I rub her wrists, massaging the redness away.

"It's not terrible at all. It means you trust me. You know that I'd never do anything to physically hurt you."

"Am I wise to do that?" There's that flicker of doubt I expected to see. She's been through hell and back. From now on I'm going to my best to make certain she only receives the love and passion she deserves.

"Giada. I'd do anything and everything to keep you from harm. That's why you're here in the first place. I left you in the care of a man I'd trust my life with even though I've been totally jealous the entire time."

"Jealous? You thought I'd sleep with him?"

"No, but he got to be in your presence while I missed you like crazy. Come here." I hug her close to me so her body's resting on mine.

"That was amazing." She clings to me, rubbing her hand over my chest. This feels too good to be true.

I run my hand down her back, then twirl my fingers around the bottom of her hair, curling it and letting go repeatedly. "Tell me about it. How are you feeling? Honestly, I hope I didn't hurt you."

She leans up on her elbows and blushes. "Only at first. There's a world of difference in size."

"Ha. That's for sure. I'm sorry." I don't want Rafael in our minds after what we did, but it's a truth that can't be avoided. Honestly, I regret nothing.

"Don't be. After I stretched wider, I came so quickly that I'm aching to do it again." She bites her lip and reaches down over my shaft. I'm still hard as fuck because that's the way I've been since I met her.

I groan, digging my teeth into my lip, straining to stop from shooting off like a teenager. "Then climb on up, baby. He's ready to go."

"But Joey might be back soon," she reminds me. Frankly, I don't give two fucks right now.

"Then you better keep your voice down. I don't want him hearing you come." I grab her hand and yank her up to straddle me. She rolls her pussy over my cock, teasing me until I lift her up and then down, impaling her on my thick shaft. "I've already been jealous of all the time you spent together," I growl out through clenched teeth.

"You have nothing to be jealous about." Giada moans, rolling her baby-carrying hips and squeezing her walls around my cock. "He hardly spoke to me unless it was to tell me to behave."

"Good. Enough about him. Ride me before I bend you over and fucking destroy your pussy."

"Yes, Santino," she moans, bouncing up and down with her ass slapping on my thighs. Her juices start to coat my cock, making it easy for her to take me deep and fast.

Suddenly, she pulls off my cock and slides down to taste us both. She sucks the tip in, causing me to jolt upward into a sitting position. Watching her greedily swallow me down deep, I lose it and thrust my fingers into her hair and take control.

"Fuck, Giada. Suck me, baby. Taste us both." With a roaring growl, my cum shoots straight down her slender throat. She swallows and keeps sucking, getting me hard again.

I flip her onto her back and drive into her pussy over and over until she's screaming out my name, clinging to me as she comes.

We lay there in the sweaty mess we created, and I feel so fucking happy that I can't even explain it. All my life I waited to get even with my brother only to fall in love with Giada. It's going to piss him off even more than I ever hoped, but she's more to me than just an opportunity for revenge. She's everything I've ever wanted in a wife. My heart and soul know that she's the only one and it'll always be that way.

Chapter Seventeen

Giada

He wraps me up with the blanket after closing the bedroom door. "Let's rest a little bit. You look exhausted."

With a smiling sigh, I say, "I can't imagine why. Please tell me you're not going to leave me the second I fall asleep."

"I'm not going anywhere." He kisses my lips and then turns off the lights.

He snuggles up with me, cradling me until we wake up four hours later.

A knock at the door stirs me awake. I move, and Santino isn't lying next to me. If it wasn't for the deep ache in my pussy, I'd believe I dreamed of it all. Shit. I look around the room, and there's no sign that he's even been in the room. So he fucked me and rushed out. I'm such a pathetic idiot.

The door opens and it's Santino, carrying in a food tray. "I thought."

"I know. I told you I wasn't leaving."

"But you will eventually, and then I'm going to be forced to stay here, right?"

"I want to say that's not the truth, but there's lots of issues right now and it's not safe."

"Fine. If you leave without me, I won't be staying here anymore. I'll do whatever I can to get away for good. I'm not going to be drugged again and left on my own." I'd had enough of the bait and switch. He has drugged me twice. The first time I was grateful. The second was hurtful. I can't take that again. It's not respect or love and that's what I want from him.

"Damn it, Giada. Do you think that I really want to leave you here?" He thrusts his hands through his hair, and then down his face.

"I don't know. I guess getting easy access to pussy might be the only reason you'd want to take me back home."

"Enough. Eat your food. Come talk to me when you're feeling less pissy and we can talk." He storms out of the room, but he doesn't close the door. Angry and hurt, I grumble under my breath before getting out of bed to get dressed. I snatch up a piece of bacon, biting into it like a starving dog, almost laughing at myself at the visual I'm presenting. It calms me down for a moment, and I go into the bathroom to freshen up after swiping another piece of bacon.

I turn on the shower, taking off his tee shirt and looking in the mirror. My body is marked up with his fingerprints and bites. God, I can't believe how incredible it felt. Closing my eyes and shaking my head, I try to put that behind me. I can't live like this, no matter how good he makes me feel when I'm in his arms.

"What am I going to do?" I sigh, knowing that I don't have an answer. I've been as patient as I can be about waiting for his return, and he's leaving me again. How can I wait? How can I run away? My chest burns and I'm not sure why. I've never felt like this before, and I'm not sure what it is. Finally turning off the water, I step out and wrap my hair in a towel and another around my chest.

I'm so exhausted that I just want to give in and do whatever Santino wants, but I also don't want to be without him. Picking out a light, summery dress, I dry off and then slip on some undergarments. I love the soft feel of the dress as it slides down my skin. He did have a lot of nice things ordered for me. They've been coming every single day. More and more clothes, as if I'm going to be living here forever.

I finally put myself together, brushing my long, dark brown hair and bundling it up into a nice clean ponytail. Feeling refreshed, I grab my plate of almost uneaten food and walk out. I follow the footsteps and see Santino pacing back and forth, running his hands through his hair.

Setting the plate down on the counter gets his attention. He lifts his head up, and I can see the fatigue and fear in his eyes, but not for long. As soon as he takes in my appearance, a smile crosses his face that threatens to undo my resolve.

"You look so beautiful, Giada. Please come and sit down."

"I'm not sure I want to do that. I have a feeling I'm not going to like anything you have to say."

"Probably, but still, there's a lot to tell you." There's a haunted look in his eyes that makes me want to comfort him. I take a seat, and he sits next to me.

I brace myself for whatever he has to say because I'm sure I'm not going to like it. "Give it to me."

"First, the reason I sent you here in the first place was

because Rafael was accusing me of taking you," he confesses.

I have so many questions, but the first one shoots from my mouth like word vomit. "So why did you drug me instead of telling me?"

"Would you have gone quietly? You already said you didn't trust me." I blush, remembering just that. "So I did what I had to do to keep you safe. A day after you were gone, they came with the cops to search the house."

"Can they do that?"

"They had a warrant, claiming I was the last person outside of the household to see you. Anyways, my staff made sure that any traces of you were gone. Things only got worse: hidden cameras, poison, shootings. My lawyer has just woken up from a coma. We were shot at on our way to the office."

"Oh my God." I grab his arm and rub around his bicep. "Were you shot?"

He nods. "Just grazed, but that's why I don't want to take you back. It's not like I don't want you by my side. It's just fucking dangerous. Seriously dangerous." I want to tell him he's being overly protective, but I know who we're dealing with. Still, the thought of being away from him for another day crushes me.

"I don't care. As an adult, I'm allowed to leave legally. It's not like Rafael can drag me back to him. I don't even understand why he wanted me in the first place."

"Because you're beautiful and he's like his father, taking something precious and ruining it."

"I'm sorry that your mother has been married to him for all these years. I guess you never know the true person until you can't get away from them."

"She knew the real him. She married him to keep me.

Marchetti isn't my real father. He killed my father and forced my mother to marry him."

"Oh shit. I don't even know how to process that."

"Trust me, I'm still coming to terms with it all. My father had been a good man. I think that's what pissed off Rafael Sr. when it came to me. He saw the same thing in me and hated that I was just like my true father."

I wrap my arms around him and hug him. "I'm sorry, Santino."

"Thank you, tesoro." He kisses my temple sweetly and I know he's a better man than I've given him credit for.

"I still want to come back with you."

"I don't think it's a good idea."

"You know they're going to eventually find out where you went and maybe even wait until you leave Joey and me here before striking."

A cloud comes over his face as he tenses up. He cups my face, stroking my cheek. "I'm taking you with me, but I want you to know that if you don't listen to me, I'll be sending your sexy ass off somewhere else. I can't risk losing you." It's that moment, the look in his eyes, those words uttered with so much emotion that it finally truly hits me. I'm not just a pawn in his revenge game. He loves me.

"I'll behave."

He flips me onto his lap so that my knees fall to the sides of his thighs. "If you don't, I still have the cuffs."

"Don't threaten me with a good time, Santino."

"Just good? I'm rusty."

"Well, then, maybe some more practice will help," I whisper against his neck. He responds by thrusting his hips upward, and his thick cock teases my pussy. He reaches under my dress and squeezes my ass, kneading it with his big strong hands.

"Sounds very good, Giada. Let him out, baby." I

unbutton his pants and pull out his cock, feeling his meaty flesh in my hands. He's hard and thick. I want him inside me, but I want him in my mouth even more. I slide off his lap and he opens his legs so I can fit between them. Stroking him up and down before swiping my tongue over his tip, I take the bead of cum for my own. A deep rumble comes from his chest, and his hands slide into my hair. I moan, sucking his shaft in, taking him halfway down.

"Fuck, Giada. That's it, take it down deep. Choke on it for your man. You're mine." I moan, sliding one hand between my thighs to strum my aching core. "Are you playing with your cunt? Let me see." I turn slightly, giving him a better angle of my slit. "Give me it." He pulls me off his cock and flips me onto the sofa, throwing my legs over his shoulders, and devours my pussy. His scruff scrapes against my skin, adding to the pleasure of his attack. I grind my mound in his face as I completely lose control. My orgasm spirals out of control as I fuck his mouth.

He doesn't hesitate more than a second to adjust his position, propelling his cock deep inside of me, stretching me wide. I cling to him with my hands cupping his neck, dragging him down for a kiss.

"Mine," he growls before crushing his lips to my own. "Fuck, you're so perfect, Giada. Come for me. I want to feel your tiny pussy fluttering around my cock before I fill you with my sons."

Oh goodness, I nearly come from the sound of his voice, but it's the image of having his babies that sends me over the edge. "I'm coming, Santino. Give it to me," I shout, tossing my head onto the sofa pillow.

"Here you go, tesoro," he grunts, slamming his cock deep until he comes inside of me. Stilling, he closes his eyes and fills me up. God, he's gorgeous. "I'll do whatever I can to protect you." He places the gentlest kiss on my lips, and I'm a goner. I think I'm in love.

He carries me back to the bedroom after adjusting his pants. "Come. We have a lot of packing to do."

"We're leaving today?"

"Yes. Sorry, but I have to get back. Despite all the other antics, I have a company to manage and I need to keep my mother safe."

"Okay. Let me freshen up and I'll clear the bathroom."

"Okay, tesoro." I love when he calls me that. I blush while walking into the bathroom. I could lose my heart to him. I hope he's as serious as he claims to be.

Chapter Eighteen

Santino

Joey and I pack up the car, while Giada does a last-minute check of the place. "How much of that did you see?" I heard his footsteps come and retreat earlier.

"Not much. Just her sliding to her knees. I didn't see anything else." That's the smart answer. I already knew he didn't come into the room all the way, but that's because he saw us. I'm going to have to be a little more careful at the house. Giada's only for me to see, and the shouts of pleasure are for my ears only.

"Good. You're a good man, Joey." I'd punch him in his balls if he walked all the way into the room. Although I do like that he saw that she wanted to please me and that she sure did. Fuck, I'm hard thinking about how willingly she drops to her knees or lets me devour her. When I told her I was going to put my son in her, she creamed so fucking hard that I knew she wanted the same thing.

I walk back in and scoop Giada into my arms. "Ready, beautiful?"

"Yes, handsome. Let's get out of here before I make you carry me back to bed."

"That is quite tempting," I growl, stealing a kiss. I'd love nothing more than to take her back to bed and fuck her until neither of us could move, but I refuse to make us an easy target.

Once we're settled in the car, Joey takes off. "Do you have to go into the office a lot or can you work from home?"

"At this point, it'll probably be fifty-fifty. With everything going on, it's not that smart to spend a great deal of time in the office." After what happened to Dimitri I know it's not wise.

"So am I going to be locked in my room all day?" She has no idea how much that hurts me to lock her away. She's too special to lose and right now there are a lot of people willing to take my sweet treasure.

"No, I've added a lot more security to the house, but I can't promise you can go outside. I can't risk your safety out in the open." She nods, processing it all. I can see she's nervous, so I give her hand a reassuring squeeze.

The drive to the airport has such a spectacular view that I wish we could have spent more time here together. Looking over at her, I see the smile on her face, and I want it forever, but the danger is real.

I can't believe I'm taking her back with me, but I can't stand to be apart anymore. Am I being selfish? I'm still not sure, but she wants to be at my side, and I can't think of anything better than that feeling of knowing she's with me.

Giada's going to have triple the security and of course, I'll be with her almost all the time.

I squeeze her hand, getting her attention. "You're going to do everything I tell you, understood?"

"Yes, Santino. I promised you. I obeyed them."

"Yes, but you know that I won't hurt you." Her face drops and I wonder if I've upset her by reminding her of the abuse. I know she didn't give herself to him willingly. She confessed that the shower had been her first orgasm. I'll do anything I can to show her that I'm not either of them.

"Hold on." I point a finger out as my phone rings.

"Hello, Mr. Bykov."

"I have some interesting news for you." There's a little humor in his voice.

"Oh yes?"

"Yes, your brother has another wife." My mouth almost dropped to the floor on that revelation.

"What?" Another wife?

He chuckles. "My men did a little snooping through Dimitri's things, and an envelope arrived today. He's married to a Marie O'Conner."

"His mistress?" I ask, already knowing that's her name, but mentally, I'm still processing it.

"Well, technically the one that lived with him…"

I cut him off before we aren't friends anymore. "If you want to live—don't finish that sentence."

With a slight pause, he says, "Oh, I see. Understood. As it is, that would make their marriage null and void."

"Are you serious?"

"Yes, that's what Dimitri had been working on. I can't read his handwriting, but I think it says, 'not real judge on wedding certificate.' Whatever that means."

"Thanks, Bykov."

"You have been a great help with the police. I will be taking Dimitri back to Russia with me tomorrow. If I do not hear from you, I will speak to you another time."

"Safe travels." He knows I'm returning today, but just in case we have someone listening; it's best to lie about travel plans as best as we can. Dimitri's just out of intensive care and can't be traveling for a few weeks at the earliest, but his enemies don't need to know that. Bykov's looking out for my mother with the rest of the team which is a godsend.

As soon as I hang up and tuck away my phone, I turn to my woman. This is important information that she needs to hear without hesitation. "There's something I need to tell you, Giada."

"What is it?" She looks nervous, and I don't like it.

"You're officially not married."

"What? Did he get a speedy divorce?" She's smiling now, but I'm sure the next part is going to take that happiness away.

"You were never legally married. His mistress has been his wife this entire time."

"What a piece of shit!"

"I'm sorry."

"Why the hell didn't he just bring her in instead of treating me like…"

"It's because I found out two days ago that his father was also sleeping with her."

"Oh God," she gasps. I see something in her eyes that makes me afraid to ask. Please tell me he didn't fuck her too.

"Did he share you?" I don't want that image in my head, but what's done is done and she's not to blame for any of it.

"No, but the day you came, Rafael's father threatened to rape me as punishment."

He's a dead man. I'm going to put a bullet in his head as soon as I get to him. "I won't let them touch you again."

"I know. Santino, kiss me please."

"You never have to beg," I growl, dropping my head down and taking her lips in a deep kiss.

"Um…we're going to miss our flight." Yanking my face away from hers, I reluctantly scowl at Joey.

"You're lucky that I like your ass. I'm ready to put bullets in bodies." Giada clings to me. "I'll be putting babies in your body," I whisper, thinking there's a possibility I already did.

"I don't know…"

"He's probably sterile."

"I was on birth control."

"What?" I look at her, feeling shocked. "How did you manage that?"

"Your mother. She's the one who gave them to me."

"I had no idea."

"Yes, what I was going to say is I don't know how long they take to stop working. I haven't had them since the night you took me from the house."

"We'll have to talk to the doc about it."

"Did he give you my test results?"

"Yes, he did. Overall you're clean from STDs and not pregnant, but you were missing key vitamins. He did say with proper nutrition that you'll be on the way to healthy levels."

"That explains the super-healthy, colorful meals."

"That, and it's not like there are many fast food places on the island."

"I wish we could have spent more time together on the island."

"Soon. I promise."

We board the plane, and I sit her next to me. After another security check, we take off. Joey sits in the aisle across from us and further down. I want Giada all alone. The plane is Bykov's and he let me use it. Learning that

Giada was restless turned me into a caged tiger. I had to get to her before she did anything stupid.

My phone rings, and it's my office. I have a conference call to take and Giada decides to nap. Once it's over, I carry her back into the plane's bed and cradle her in my arms. We had a long night of lovemaking that we're both exhausted from.

I don't realize that I fell asleep with her until Joey knocks. "We're about to land."

"Okay." He nods and leaves us. "Wake up, beautiful. We have to take our seats."

"Okay." She yawns and stretches. God, I want her so badly that my cock throbs against my slacks. Helping her sit up, she wakes up a little more and then we finally make it to our seats.

"I'll be leading us off the plane. Several of the guards are already waiting for us, and we're entering a secure tarmac," Joey informs us as we buckle ourselves in.

"Don't be nervous."

"You know this is the first time I've ever been on a plane that I was awake for?"

"Are you serious?"

"Yes, I was kept a prisoner my whole life." She says it so nonchalantly that I almost think she's kidding, but the look in her eyes says otherwise. It's as if she's reliving those shitty memories.

"Stop it. Stop whatever you're thinking. Just stop it, Giada."

"Sorry, Santino." She looks at me with wonder in her eyes, and I can't stop myself. Cupping her cheek, I take her mouth, kissing her until we're both panting. I hear a grunt and see an eye roll from Joey. Flipping him off, I kiss her again. I could do this all damn day long. She's everything and more to me. Once we get home, I'm going to verify the information from Bykov and then marry Giada myself.

The plane lands, and we deplane about fifteen minutes later when given the all clear. The thought of spending the rest of my life looking over my shoulder is unacceptable. Something had to give.

Chapter Nineteen

Santino

It's been a week since I brought Giada back home, and it was a smart decision. Being without her was hard, but leaving her would have been excruciating. We haven't heard or seen anyone from the Marchetti family. They have been quiet, but we all know it's just a matter of time before they greet us with a round of violence.

As I'm getting ready for work, Giada stretches her arms up in the air, letting the sheet fall from her fabulous tits. "Good morning, beautiful."

"Good morning. You're going into the office?"

"Yes. I have an important meeting this morning, so I might as well make the most of it while I'm there."

"Of course. Maybe your mom and I will have some girl time today."

"I wish you two could go out to do girl things."

"It's okay. Just be careful." She climbs up onto her knees and grabs my tie, dragging me to her for a kiss. Thrusting my fingers into her hair, I slip my tongue in her mouth. My phone buzzing is the only thing keeping me from fucking her right now.

"Sorry, tesoro. I have to go. Please stay away from the front door and the windows. I know it's crazy, but for me."

"Of course." I give her a little peck before rushing out of our bedroom. God, I'm addicted.

Joey drives me to the office with two guards driving behind me. Once we get inside, I go to my office and get to work. The receptionist who put in a listening device had already been canned when I came back from the island. HR brought in a temp who has been screened thoroughly.

I don't know the girl, and I don't want to get to know her. She's only here to do her job, so as long as her ass stays out of my office, I'm thoroughly pleased with her work so far.

I'm more than halfway through my day and my meetings are all done. While I really want to go home, I have to catch up on some paperwork. I know that I have little to no control when it comes to Giada, so I'll end up forgetting work and have her on my desk instead.

My alarm on my phone goes off, and I see it's from the front desk. A cop just came barging through to see me. I sent Joey on an errand for me, so he's not around, but I prepare myself for this bullshit. I turn on all the cameras and another recording device under the chair in front of my desk.

The second "the cop" barges through my door, I stand up behind my desk, preparing for the war, but playing it cool all the same. "It's so good to see you, Rafael. What brings you to see me? Run out of goons to do it for you? Is there a bomb in my car?"

He smiles and takes a seat in front of my desk. "No. Can't I see my brother?"

"Brother?" I chuckle. "What do you want?" Just seeing

his face makes me want to bash his skull in. The thought of him touching Giada, hurting her, stealing her joy drives me to want him dead more than any other fucked-up thing he's done to me.

"My wife back." I've tried to let go of the idea that he'd ever touched my woman, but he's only digging his own grave.

I laugh at that because she's not his wife, and he's about to learn that I know his dirty, fucked-up secret. I adjust my suit and sit down. "Where is Marie at? I didn't know she left you too."

He twists his head. "So you found out about that?" He's trying to hide his anger, but I can read him like a book.

"Yes, I did, and a lot more."

"Well, you weren't listening to my calls then because Marie is no longer my wife, so Giada is all mine. I know you have my wife."

"First, legally speaking, Giada is not your wife and never was. What did you do to Marie?" I'm betting he killed her.

He smiles. "She paid for her infidelity." Oh the irony. "Giada is my wife, and you have her. I know it." He leans forward, trying to look tough with me, but I'm more scared of my own shadow than I've ever been scared of him.

"Oh really? How do you *know* that?" I challenge, wondering how much he actually knows or if he's trying to con me.

"She's got a tracker in her. Did you think I'd not know where she was at all times?"

I scoff. "Bullshit." I lean back in my chair as if I don't have a care in the world. At this moment, I know that we're about to go toe to toe, but it's been a long time coming. We may be blood, but we aren't family.

"You're a liar. Nice try, Rafael. I'm not one to try that with."

He can see that I'm not budging on this one bit. I'm not the gullible fuck he sent away. "You got smarter in prison."

"I'm glad you noticed. It means you're not entirely an imbecile."

"You think you're so fucking special, don't you? You always thought you were."

"No, I'm just not a psychopath like yourself." I smirk at the bastard, loving the way he's becoming unnerved. "What do you really want, Rafael?"

"I told you I want you to give me back my wife."

"Ha. Are you trying to find another reason to put me back in prison? Because I'll see you there first. I've already got enough on you and your father for you to spend the rest of your lives there. Is that why you tried to kill my lawyer?"

"The lawyer we had nothing to do with. We don't have problems with the Russians, so we never touched him. Although you, on the other hand, I'd rather see you in a pine box, gladly."

"You first, Rafael," I snarl, standing up.

He whips out the gun he hid under his jacket. He goes to pull the trigger, but he has no idea how long I've been waiting for this moment. I twist my body to the side as the bullet cracks the window behind me. It's strong glass so it doesn't shatter, but I make a beeline in his direction.

As he goes to shoot again, I rush him, sending him to the ground with my arms around his throat, choking him. The gun falls from his hand, but he can still reach it as he stretches for it, so I drill my elbow into his wrist. He hollers out in pain, making me smile.

"God, I love this more than I should." He kicks me in

Stolen Wife

the thigh, missing my balls, which I'm sure his little ass was going for.

"You need to die," he croaks out.

I slam my fist into his face. "You first."

He flails his good arm at me, but it's too weak, so he reaches for the gun. His fingers just touch the grip when I wrench it from him. I lean in and say, "I have her and I'm fucking her every damn night."

"You son of a bitch." He grabs my arm, trying to wrestle the gun out of my hand, but I'm stronger and pull the trigger, shooting him in the chest. My security team arrives as the shot goes off. I fall backward, leaning against my desk as I catch my breath.

"Are you okay, boss?" Joey asks.

"Yeah." Joey offers his hand and I stand up, setting the gun on the desk. "Call the police." I look at my brother and know that a medic is useless. His eyes are wide open and his expression is vacant.

The ambulance and the police arrive right after each other. The medics work on Rafael for two minutes, but they know it's too late. He wasn't worth saving anyway. He killed the only woman he claimed to love.

The lead officer approaches me and says, "I'm Detective Randall. Mr. Marchetti—"

I cut him off. "Actually, the last name is Benedetti. I had it changed legally yesterday."

"You're arguing over a name, and I have a dead body in the middle of your office," he scolds me, narrowing his brows at me as if I'm supposed to be intimidated.

"And? I killed the bastard in self-defense." I step away from my desk so they can retrieve the weapon. "You can see he's been shot with his own gun, and if you look closely you'll see the nice damage to my window over there." I point to the giant crack in the window with the bullet hole at the center of it. "If that's not enough, I recorded Rafael's conversation with me before I did the world a service."

"I just can't believe you don't have any remorse for killing your own brother."

"You know about the poisoning, right? The threats, my lawyer in the hospital fighting for his life, and to top it off, this bastard sent me to prison."

"He was involved?" he questions as if it comes as a surprise. Most really are under the impression that we were a cohesive unit, but we were the furthest thing from a family. The police and the Marchetti family have managed to keep it out of the papers for everyone to see, but there has always been strife between us all. They load my brother on the gurney, zipping up the body bag.

"Yes, but then again, I can't expect you all to do your job. If it's not enough, you can view security cameras that show this asshole bypassing my security with this." I toss the badge at him.

The guy turns white as a ghost, looking up at me with a new sadness and chokes out, "Do you know this detective has been missing for nearly a week?"

Shit. Not that I put it past Rafael at all. "Well, sorry. I don't even know who's badge that is."

"It's Detective Morel."

"What? Detective Morel? Shit. Those sons of bitches. They killed him because he told me about my real father. I look over at what remains of my brother in the body bag. "Sorry that you can't question him now, but if I were you, I'd contact his father; he might know about it." The sound of Rafael's phone interrupts us.

I read the message from Marchetti*: **Have you done it? Is he out of the way? I'm ready to get her back.***

I show it to the detective and then my own phone goes

off. It's from my security team. Shit. "Wow, that's all the evidence I need to make an arrest on your father," the detective says.

The bastard isn't my father. "Hold on. First, he's not my father. Second, he's going to my house to try to steal my mother back."

"We can get to her first," he says.

"No, you can't. He's waiting. This is from my security team." I show them footage the team just sent me. The fuck is waiting for her outside of his car, staring at one of my guards from across the road to the gate entrance. "Is there a way to get her out safely?" I ask.

"Not without drawing attention."

Nodding, I say, "He's not above killing them all. I have a plan." I grab Rafael's phone and type. ***The bastard's not going to be a problem anymore. He has that bitch as well. I'm going to go get her. Wait for me. We'll break the sad news to them together.***

"Wow, you're a lot more devious than they give you credit for."

"They killed my real father, sent me to prison, and stole the bride who should have been mine. There's no limit to my revenge."

Suddenly he stiffens by my side. "So you plan on taking their place?"

I look at him and scoff, clearly insulted. "Their empire can rot in hell. I want nothing to do with it, and you can tell your friends that too. I don't want any part of the mafia, but I won't hesitate to protect what's mine."

"Understood. Now, I'm going to arrest him if you want to follow."

"He probably has men outside the building out of the camera frames."

"Okay. We'll play this right."

Chapter Twenty

Giada

As soon as Santino's gone for the day, I get in the shower and get dressed. Without him here, there's no reason to lie in bed. Once I'm ready with a hint of makeup on my face, I walk downstairs the back way to the kitchen.

"Good morning, Giada," Santino's mom says.

"Good morning, Rita, Mom." She's not my mom by blood, but she's the only mother to show me the love a mother should have.

"Did you sleep well?" Mom asks with a smirk on her face.

"It was a wonderful night, even if I hardly slept." I giggle. A new life has been breathed into me. I can't believe all that's changed in the past twenty-four hours. There are plenty of changes since Santino first walked into my life, and I hope more to come.

"I bet you're hungry." Rita slides over a full breakfast.

"Thanks. I am." I hop on a stool and ask, "How are you ladies this morning?"

"I'm trying to keep this woman over here from losing her mind. I told her that Santino's not going to let her husband get her, but she's worried."

"I'm not scared for myself but for Santino. He's strong, but they are ruthless. Nothing is going to stop them from going at him, even if I went back to Rafael." She's exactly right. There's no doubt about that when it comes to those bastards. I hate them to no end and want both of them dead.

"He's well protected. I wish I could tell you that it's going to be okay. Me more than anyone wants him to come home safe." I press my hand to my stomach, feeling nauseous at the idea that he could die.

"I know. We need to pray that he'll be safe. The detective on my first husband's case wanted to do a formal interview with me, but I'm guessing that he hasn't gotten into contact with Santino yet." I've learned so much more about her past over the past week than I did the entire time I knew her. It's way more tragic than mine. At least mine started off brutally awful, but her happiness came and went and she suffered the last thirty years.

"Hopefully, you two can fill this house with laughter and joy and a bunch of grandbabies for me to love."

"I'm sure Santino's going to try." I smile, finally taking my first bite of the eggs.

"I'm thinking that there are four extra bedrooms upstairs perfect for babies. You might need a bigger house."

"How many babies do you expect us to have?" I bite a piece of bacon. God, I love bacon.

"Is six too greedy?"

I nearly spit it out at her. "Yes."

She waves my answer off, shaking her head. "Well, at least I didn't say a full dozen." She grins, taking a sip of her coffee. There's nothing to do but shake my head. I'll be happy with any babies we have together. It's more than I could have ever hoped for.

"Yeah, well, we'll see. I don't know about the football team you want, but I'm just happy to have a chance at even one little Santino." Tears well up in her eyes and I feel awful for her, but she stands up and wraps her arms around me. "Thank you for giving him the chance to prove his love."

"He's my hero." *Even if he's a bossy ass sometimes.*

"We need to start picking out baby furniture," she squeals, jumping up and down.

"We don't even know if I'm pregnant or can ever get pregnant."

"I just have a feeling. Finish your food and we can start looking at some online stores." She walks out of the kitchen and into the main sitting area. Several guards are around the house and in almost every room. We don't have a lot of privacy, but they all seem like pretty cool people.

Rita's breakfast is fabulous, but I'm so full that I get up and empty my plate.

"Thank you for breakfast. It was incredible, as always."

"That's what I'm here for." After putting my plate in the sink, she wraps her arms around me. "He's going to be okay. He's tougher than they are, and smarter."

"Giada," Mom shouts from the other room. "You have to see this."

Shaking my head, I walk to the kitchen door. "Good luck, Giada. She's been talking about babies for days now."

"Hopefully we've been making babies for days." I push it open and go into the living room where she's got a laptop open, scrolling through baby room ideas.

For the next few hours we stay glued to these sites, finding cute baby rooms that I want. I love almost all of them. I can't decide and honestly, until I'm pregnant, all of this is moot, but it's better than sitting around waiting for bad news to hit us.

It's well after lunch when I can hear excessive movement around the house. We were watching some soap operas when the news comes on. "Shots fired at an office building. It's the second shooting at this building in as many weeks. We don't have any details, but from the lack of rushing or staging outside the building, we can assume that it's already been subdued. The medics are leaving and the coroner has appeared on the scene." They walk up to Joey who's holding a bag in his hand and just going toward the building. "Sir, can you tell us what's going on?"

"No." He pushes past them and the police officers, showing his badge and whispering something. Tears are flowing down my face as I wonder what's going on.

Suddenly Martin and Angela are in the room. "Ladies, we need to take shelter in the specialized room."

"Oh my goodness. It's Rafael, isn't it?"

"Yes, but we're going to secure you and inform Santino."

"But the shooting?"

"He's okay as far as we know. We just received word from Joey. Please accompany us to where we can keep you safe." They are insistent and I can't take it right now. I'm so freaked out about Santino that I can hardly concentrate on actually breathing.

"Why can't they just leave us alone?" I sob into my hands.

Mom wraps her arms around me and kisses my hair. "Because they can't stand losing their possessions. That's all we were to them. A possession that they didn't care for, but hell if they wanted anyone else to have it."

It takes me a minute to calm myself down and focus on

the path ahead as we move into a safe room that Santino had built over the first few days I'd been on the island.

We go down into the room and wait for word on Santino. I need to know he's okay. Goodness, I don't know what I'd do if he doesn't come home to me. We are just getting started on our happily ever after and I can't lose him.

For the next hour, it feels like nothing but a waiting game. One I don't like playing. All I want is Santino. I don't even have a cell phone to check up on him.

I close my eyes and think of him and the vows we spoke the other day.

"Giada, will you do me the honor in marrying me?"

"Marry you? Why would you want that?"

"Because I know you're the one for me and I can't imagine a life without you in it. I knew it the second I crept into the room and snatched you up."

"Yes. Yes I'll marry you."

"Thank you, Tesoro. The judge will be here in two hours."

"Are we getting married today?"

"Yes. Sorry. We can have a special wedding later, but I want you with me before someone can try to separate us ever again."

"I don't need anything special except you." He slides a diamond ring.

"This has got to be one of the shortest engagements ever."

"That's okay with me."

"What am I going to wear?"

"Rita has already thought of that. Well her and my mother, but since Rita's the only one of you that can go out, she picked up three dresses this morning."

"Oh my goodness." I kiss him hard and then run from the room to see both Rita and his mom waiting for me.

"Yes. We have to get started."

"He'll be here by five."

My two hours flew by fast, but I'm ready. Walking down the stairs with Joey, leading me to Santino, I walk up to Santino who's standing there with a smile on his face. We have a small gathering of Russian mob people and the security as our guests. They all stand as I move down the makeshift aisle with only two hours he'd made every minute count. It's perfect.

Within ten minutes it's all over and the photographer snaps photos of us. I can't believe how he managed to do all this but I'm happy. Cupping my cheeks, he presses his forehead to mine and says, "I love you, Giada."

"I love you, Santino." We kiss as if we don't have an audience and honestly I don't care who sees it. Before the judge leaves we filed all the necessary docs with the notarized and ready to be submitted for public record. We even made copies should something befall the judge before the documents are entered. Although I'm sure Santino won't let that happen.

"Congratulations, Mrs. Benedetti."

"Thank you, your honor."

He leaves as we enjoy a small cake that Rita ordered along with some fine Italian cuisine from a local restaurant. The entire time, Santino can't take his eyes off of me, and there's always a hint of a smile on it with a wink or two even when he talks to the Russians.

"Giada, Giada," Mom says, shaking me out of my memory.

"Oh no what's going on?"

"Are you okay? We lost you there for a minute. He's going to be okay. I'm sure of it."

"Thank you. I was lost in a very happy memory." We hug and wait for news.

Chapter Twenty-One

Santino

"Romo, what brings you here?" I ask as we step out of my office to go to the parking garage. I don't want the media or my father to know that I'm alive, so this is the only way to go about it.

"I heard the call on the radio. Are you okay, Santino?"

I still can't trust him, but I'm getting a little closer to it. The next few hours will tell me a lot about who he really is. "I am. Now's not the time to retell what happened. He's on the way to get my mother."

"Then let's go. I've already pinned those guys who were outside the building. I saw them lingering. One of them was the one at your house the other day, so they're all on the way to the station."

I remember that bastard. Faustino. I want to rip his eyeballs out and shove them down his throat. Giada told me what he said to her and what Rafael had planned once she gave him a baby, which gave me more pause. He would have killed her like he did Marie if she fucked anyone else. There's no way he'd share. It's just who these guys were. It had to be a setup to kill two birds with one stone.

Knowing he's locked up means he doesn't have eyes on the building to see us leave. "Thank fuck. I don't want Marchetti to have a heads up that we're coming for him."

I jump in my vehicle with Joey at my side. I send Martin a message to take them to the safe room until I come back.

We pull up to the house and there's Rafael Sr. waiting in his car with two guys. They're armed.

We don't get too close, and he doesn't see me yet. "Mr. Marchetti, please step out of the car and put your hands up." He surrenders easily, which takes me by surprise. "Mr. Marchetti, you're under arrest for conspiracy to commit murder, the attempted abduction of Mrs. Marchetti, and the unlawful imprisonment of Giada Avanti."

"Her name is Marchetti."

"Actually, let me correct both of you. Her name is Giada Benedetti. She's my wife, legally." He looks as if he sees a ghost. My shirt's still splattered with blood, and I hadn't thought of it until his haunted expression.

"Where's Rafael?"

I smile and then suck in some air. "Oh shit. I'm going to have to break the news to Mom. Damn, she's going to be crushed." I watch as his face shifts from heartbroken to pure rage.

"You killed my son, you fucking bastard."

"Yeah, well. It was either him or me. You bet on the wrong horse. Besides, you killed my father."

"You're a dead man." He snarls, attempting to break free from the cuffs.

"You keep trying, and I'm not the one who's going to be six feet under soon. I wonder if they're going to let you out for his funeral. Well, I suppose someone needs to do the planning." I shrug and smirk.

"You'll pay for this."

"I already have." I walk away, hating how awful I'm being about my brother's death. Despite it all, he was my brother. We grew up together, even though he hated me and I didn't trust him.

I finally make it into the house and into the safe room. As soon as the door slides open, Giada is in my arms with her legs wrapped around my waist, kissing my face. "Baby. Baby. I'm okay."

"We heard on the news that there was a shooting at an office building. And I saw Faustino outside the building, so I thought they came after you. Then Martin secured us in here."

"They did come after me." I hold up my hand to interrupt Giada. "Mom, I'm sorry, but Rafael is dead."

"I know. I knew that only one of you would come out alive if something like this happened. It's terrible, but I hoped it would be you." She hugs me and sobs. For all that he was, he was still her son. Her baby just like I was. "I wish Rafael had done better with him. I wish he would have let me raise him as I raised you."

"He needed someone to follow in his footsteps."

"Oh goodness, he's going to come here shooting up the house."

"No. He's been arrested outside the house. He was coming to get you." She fell to the chair and sat down.

After a minute, she cries into her hands. "My heart aches so painfully. God, I cannot reconcile the feelings in me."

"I'm sorry, Mom." Giada moves to my mother and hugs her. I see the tears in my woman's eyes, and I try not to let jealousy seep in.

"You can hate him. It's okay, Giada," my mother says.

"I'm not crying for him. I'm crying for you and the way this all could have been avoided." I lean over and touch her shoulder. Both women separate and Giada clings to me. "I'm sorry for what you had to do."

"Thank you, my love. I'm sorry, too. If only things had been different."

"Santino, I hate to interrupt, but the police would like a word with you."

"Which one?"

"Randall."

"Martin, protect them with your life." I give Giada a hard kiss and brush her stomach before walking out.

It takes me another twenty minutes with the officers and their questions. They want to talk to my mother and wife, but it will have to wait. I'm about to walk inside when a woman in a suit approaches us. "Hello, Mr. Benedetti, is it?"

"Yes, and you are?"

"Sorry. I'm DA Erin Lowe." Joey appears next to me all of a sudden, and I see something different in his stance.

"Excuse me. I'm here to have a private conversation with Mr. Benedetti."

"I'm his personal guard, so…"

"Whatever. We've reviewed the evidence on the scene and the police were given a copy of the audio from staff. A copy will be also given to the district attorney's office. However, from the footage and the audio, it's clear he came in to kill you and you fought over the weapon. We've decided that no charges will be filed against you."

"Thank you."

"But I must warn you that it's not over yet. You and Mrs. Benedetti must be careful. There are still loyal puppies to the Marchettis and should Marchetti get out on bail, I expect him to find a way to get to you. We can provide you with additional security if needed."

"No, I have plenty on my staff and frankly, I have less trust in the justice system than I do in actual crooks. Is there anything else I need to be made aware of?"

"Yes. This morning we discovered the bodies of six men and a woman in a mass grave just outside of the city limits. One of the men was Detective Morel, and the other men worked for your father and the woman was Marie O'Conner."

"Rafael's wife..."

"Yes, we heard the audio. I'm assuming both men committed the killings, but as of right now the audio only links Rafael Jr. Also, due to the conversation you had with Detective Morel, we are charging Rafael Sr. with the murder of both Morel and Santino Benedetti Sr."

"My mother will be pleased."

"That's all for now, Mr. Benedetti." She looks at Joey and scowls. "You stay out of trouble, Joseph."

"Whatever, sweetheart." He winks at her.

"Is there something I missed?"

"She's the one who put me in prison and she's the one who got me out, even if she won't admit to it. I want to bend her sexy ass over and remind her of how good our one night was."

"Oh shit. There's a lot more to that, but I need to take a shower and comfort my wife."

"Lucky bastard." We walk inside the gate, and security shuts and locks it up. I'm tired and need to take out my confusion about what I've done with my mouth between my wife's legs.

Chapter Twenty-Two

Giada

Two months later

It feels so good to be out of the house. We've only been out a handful of times since Rafael's death. It's not that safe, but we had enough and promised we'd take as many guards as Santino wanted as long as we can have a nice mother-daughter day. His mom has truly become like a real mother to me. I'm surrounded by wall-to-wall security, but Mom and I are getting our nails and feet done.

"I need to thank Santino for this special treat."

"I know, right? I'm so happy right now. For months I've been locked up, and now I'm free and madly in love." I giggle as we sit with our feet soaking in the hot water.

"Giada?" I look over and see my actual mother and a woman I don't know. Well, woman is hardly an accurate description. She looks younger than me. "What are you doing here?"

"I'm getting my nails done. What does it look like?" The woman has a lot of nerve coming to even speak to me.

"Is that any way to talk to your mother?"

"You're not my mother," I remind her. She gave up that right the second she pawned me off on that monster.

"And this puttana is your mother? She married her husband's murderer and helped him set up the D'Angelos. She belongs in prison too." I jump out of my chair to knock this bitch out, but Santino's mom puts her hand on my arm and shakes her head. I suppose she's right.

"Ma'am, you're going to have to leave." One of my guards grabs her around the arm.

"We have an appointment."

"Not anymore," he adds.

He's about to lead them out when Mom says, "Never mind. They can stay. I'm not going to let her, or anyone, get the better of me. She's the one who sold her daughter into a violent, loveless marriage because she was having an affair with my soon-to-be ex-husband."

She gasps, and I'm shocked. Nothing about Rafael Marchetti had been good looking, so how did he get all these women to cheat on their husbands? "You don't know anything."

I roll my eyes at her and let a guffaw slips past my lips. "Whatever. That expression on your face says enough, but young lady, I'd watch out. They traffic women. I know because I was one and this woman gave birth to me." The young lady pulls away from my incubator and rushes out of the building. "One less victim, Mrs. Avanti?" I tease.

"Bitch, you will pay."

"I already have." She leaves in a rush. That poor girl needs to get far away before they catch her, and this time it won't be some nice charity they do. She'll be drugged and turned over quickly.

I call my guard over and say, "Please check on that young lady. I don't want her injured too." He nods and goes to find the young lady. I turn to my mother-in-law and apologize. "I'm sorry about her."

"No, Giada. I'm the one who should be sorry for you. You had a terrible family and were forced to marry my son."

"I know, but if it hadn't been Rafael, it would have been one of the D'Angelos, and I would have never met Santino. I can't change my past. I've decided that I can't be a victim forever. Rafael's just a bad relationship like many women have, or that's the way I'm going to see it because I want to be happy with Santino and the past will only get in the way."

"You're so wise for your age."

"I wish. I'm going to try to read more books and see where that goes. I only have a high school education, and I was homeschooled at that. My education was only so the state didn't ask questions. They already sewed up my life the second I grew breasts."

"Again. I'm so sorry, but I promise to be the mother and grandmother that they show on those sweet movies."

"I'm sure you will. Now, enough of this stressful nonsense. Let's enjoy being pampered."

We spend the rest of the day out and about shopping and eating lunch at a nice café. It's almost time for Santino to get out of work, so we head back to the house.

He comes home about an hour after we do, but he's looking grumpy. I'm sure they told him about the run-in with my egg donor.

"What's wrong, Santino?" I ask, brush my hand along his bicep.

"Nothing," he grunts, kissing my cheek before moving to take off his suit jacket and shoes.

"That hardly looks like nothing."

"I'm fine."

Ha. I don't believe him for a minute. "Bullshit."

"What did I tell your pretty ass about swearing?"

"I don't know. I think I need a reminder."

With a growl, he scoops me up and takes the stairs two at a time to our room. "Clothes off now," he barks as he quickly strips out of his own. He's on me like a wild animal kissing and biting while pumping into me until I'm screaming his name over and over again.

We're snuggling under the covers when I broach the subject of his mood when he came home. "So about this grumpiness?"

He leans on his elbow and forearm and says, "Denton, he shot Dimitri."

"The guy you fired?"

He nods, feeling the weight of the blame. "Yes, but he didn't do it to get at me. Denton was just looking for someone to take me out. Now it's not me he's got to worry about. It had to do with the Russians and their enemies. It was a ruse meant to have Alexei react and blame me, but their plan backfired because Bykov had common sense and a shrewdness about him that didn't allow him to overreact without thinking things through."

"Thankfully. Besides, he did seem like a nice guy when we met." He went back and forth until Dimitri was well enough to travel. Dimitri came to visit us before going to Russia for a long vacation.

"He's not a nice guy." Santino growls out of jealousy.

"I mean that he kind of is a decent guy to you. He lent you the plane to come and get me."

"You have a point," he grumbles, but there's a possessive glint in his eyes that just dares me to add fuel to that flame.

"He's kind of good looking too." He flips me onto my back and pins me to the bed just as I expected.

"Mrs. Benedetti, I'm afraid you're in need of a reminder of who you belong to and what I'll do to keep you with me forever." He reaches over into our bedroom drawer and pulls out the cuffs.

"You wouldn't," I challenge as I feel my pussy clench with desire.

"You know I will. Hands."

"No," I refuse, shaking my head to the side. He flips me onto my belly and slides my arms behind my back.

"You know that's going to cost you."

"Yep."

"You're not supposed to enjoy your punishment, my love."

"I enjoy everything with you." He lifts my ass up, wrapping one strong hand on the cuffs, restraining my wrists while the other hand guides his thick cock deep inside in one fluid motion. I feel so full from this position and I want more. I push my ass back onto his abs as he thrusts hard over and over again.

"You're mine, Giada. Now, tell me what I want to hear."

"I'm yours, Santino. Only yours."

"That's good, baby. Now come on my dick. I want to feel your release milking every last creamy drop out of my balls." He leans down, planting his hands on the mattress and his chest on my back. I curve my fingers and scratch at his belly, loving the way he gets so worked up.

"Give it to me," he demands, and my pussy does his bidding, coming hard on his length. He pumps hard, shooting his cum on my pulsing walls. "So beautiful. Giada, you are so beautiful."

Epilogue

Santino

A year later

"THE MARCHETTI FAMILY HAD COLLAPSED AT THE WEIGHT *of the elder Rafael Marchetti's arrest last year. Although no one is talking, there is speculation that the hit on Marchetti had come from another crime family on the East Coast. The body had been found floating in the ravine just off the New Jersey turnpike at the Delaware Memorial Bridge. Marchetti had been awaiting trial for the murder of at least six individuals, including New York Homicide Detective Michael Morel when he'd gone missing nearly a year ago. It was believed that he fled to Italy to avoid prosecution, but with the spring thaw, two Department of Transportation workers located the body during a routine inspection on the bridge.*

"Detective Morel had been petitioning to open up the nineteen-ninety case of the murder of Santino Benedetti. The family details have been a sordid one straight out of a Hollywood movie. That's it

from outside the district attorney's office, I'm Anita Perez for GBC Television."

I click off the news and switch it to the weather. It's going to be a great day today. Spring is here, and I'm home. The news cameras are already shining outside my door.

"Sir, do you want me to shoo them away?" Martin asks, coming to stand at my side. It's been a busy morning, and I just got off the phone with the DA an hour ago before this report came on the air.

"No, I'll address them briefly." I walk out of the house with my security to the front gate. I won't open it because this isn't worth more than a minute of my time.

"Mr. Benedetti, Mr. Benedetti," the reporters shout. I raise my hand to silence them.

"I won't be taking more than a couple of questions, so make it count."

I point to one of the men in the front. "Mr. Benedetti, how are you feeling with the news of your estranged stepfather's death?"

"As most of you have heard, he's the reason my real father isn't here. My mother and I suffered a lifetime of abuse from him. So all I can say is, I'm glad the son of a bitch is dead. My family can breathe a little easier. Next question."

"Are you considered a suspect in his murder?"

"No, and I shouldn't be. I wasn't even here when he initially disappeared. I'd been on a month-long business trip in Africa with my wife. I didn't have a hand in his death, but I'm not in the least bit sorry he's gone. Now, that's all I'm going to say. The rest speaks for itself." I spin on my heel and start toward the house.

"Just one more question…" I pause and turn back around. "Do you have a clue who did it?"

"No, I don't. He had a lot of enemies. I wouldn't put it past anyone, but they deserve a fucking medal in my opinion. Have a great day."

"Congratulations on your new son."

"Thank you." Giada hadn't gotten pregnant right away. I wasn't surprised that it took several months because she'd been malnourished for months, but Giada worried there was more to it. After seeing the doctor and reading up on all the medical articles and journals, we learned that after stopping birth control it can be hard to get pregnant right away. Since she hadn't taken it for more than a year, we didn't have to wait that long for the news that she was having my baby. Two days ago she gave birth and now my wonderful tiny family is resting. I think it's time I joined them.

"Martin, I don't want to be disturbed for the rest of the day."

He grins, knowing that I'm greedy to hold my son. My father missed these moments, and I don't want to take them for granted. "Yes, sir. What about dinner?"

"I'll ask Giada what she wants. She needs her strength back."

"Sounds good. I'll let Rita know, but I can't promise she's not going to sneak up to see the little guy."

"I know. I'm sure my mom is already up there with Giada." He nods and walks away.

I open the bedroom door to see Giada on the bed, glowing as she nestles our son to her breast. My mother turns to look at me, and tears roll down her face. I walk over to her and pull her into my arms. "You look so much like your father. Sometimes it takes me by surprise. He'd be so proud of you."

"Thank you."

"I'm going to give you some time alone. I made Martin promise to take me to lunch."

"Sounds great. Take extra security."

"I will." She gives me a kiss and then leaves the room, closing the door. I direct my attention back to my wife.

"How are you feeling, tesoro?"

"I'm wonderful. Even the residual pain can't bring me down. Is everything okay?"

I kick off my shoes and climb onto the bed next to her. "Yes, I spoke to the reporters." I brush my baby boy's tiny fingers, amazed at this little miracle we made together.

"I'm sure they were itching for a story."

"Of course. I gave them a little to stir the pot, but nothing to bring them back to us. I hope they don't darken our doorstep with their bright lights and greed for gossip."

"I'm glad it was you. I probably would have bitten their heads off."

"You're a sweetheart, but even you can't hold back on your hate for him."

"Any news on his other son?"

"Yes, Marie's mother has custody of him. I'm going to see if we can liquidate all of Marchetti's assets and then give it to them. It's hard because he used a lot of it to pay his lawyers."

"Well, I know that we don't owe the boy anything, but I'd like to do something for him. It's not his fault he got stuck with a shitty family."

"You have the heart of an angel. I was thinking the same. I'm planning on setting up a small trust that he'll have access to when he reaches twenty-one."

"That sounds so wonderful. Have you ever met him?"

"No, but I hope he's going to be okay. I'd hate it if he fell into the same path as Rafael."

"Me too. It's possible with the right role models that he can have a good normal life."

"Have you spoken to his grandparents?"

"Yes, but they stopped talking to Marie two years ago when Rafael threatened them."

"Oh."

"They want him to stay completely out of the family business. Marie had been naïve and impressionable when she ran off at sixteen to New York, but Cara Mia, let's just focus on our little guy for now. I don't want these memories tainted with the past."

"Of course, my love, but someone is sleeping." She pulls him off her breast and covers herself up, to my disappointment. I love seeing her tits, which have grown even more as they fill with milk. "Getting your fill?"

"Not yet, but I suppose you can cover those delicious mounds." I drop my head and kiss her lips. "I love you so much, Giada. Thank you for my son and your love."

"I wouldn't be here without you." She softly chokes back tears.

It breaks my heart to see her cry. "I would have come for you even if it wasn't that night."

She mumbles under her breath, but I slide my hand under her chin and lift it to my gaze. I want to hear what she has to say. "What was that?"

"It would have been too late. I mean that in all seriousness. If you hadn't kidnapped me from my room, they would have killed me. They told me that very day that if I got my period again, I'd come up missing. So every day I thank goodness that you had fallen for me."

In that moment, I realized how lucky I'd truly been. I can't even fathom the thought that I could have been too late. There's no way I can picture my life without her. "I won't let anyone take you from me. Ever."

Four years later

Giada

I breathe in the warm, fresh breeze as the sun sets. Texas, I think I'm in love. It's so wonderful here. I'm so glad Santino took us away from New York and moved his company headquarters to just outside of Houston. His mother lives on the same plot of land, but in her own home. With baby number three on the way, we need all the space we can get. Michael, Carlotta, and soon-to-be-born Gio are our loves. I rub my belly, feeling his little foot destroy my abdomen. It's amazing and painful at the same time.

I feel Santino's hands slide around my waist from behind, closing over my own hand. "Sorry, tesoro. I wish I could take the pain away."

"It's fine. You know I love carrying your babies."

"Still. You should be pampered."

"I hardly do anything, my dear husband," I say, lifting up onto my toes to kiss his chin. "I love this scruff."

"Maybe we should go inside, and you can show me how much you love it."

"Now that's a fabulous idea, Mr. Benedetti." Before I can react, Santino swoops me up into his arms, cradling me as he marches back into the house. We make it through the door when his phone rings. "Give me one minute," he growls, setting me down on the settee in the foyer.

"Hello, Mom," he answers on speaker.

"Santino, you need to come quick. Michael cut himself and we need to take him to the hospital." I'm off the settee, grabbing my purse. I have to get to my babies.

"Shit, we're on our way. Call an ambulance," he barks in fear. My heart starts jumping out of my chest and my stomach hurts. The pain is different and yet all too familiar. I hope we make it to the hospital before things accelerate into a full blown labor.

"I did."

"Is it bad?" I shout over Santino's arm as we run out of the house.

"He's going to need stitches," my mother-in-law says.

We get to the house in less than two minutes and they're bringing Michael out. Santino scoops him up and sits on the porch to look at the cut on his leg. "How are you, my baby boy?"

He frowns and points to the bandage. "I'm sorry, Daddy. I wanted to be a big boy, but it hurts." He sobs against Santino's chest.

"It's my fault. I went to help Carlotta with mixing the cookie dough and I turned my back for a minute." She's crying hysterically and Martin is carrying Carlotta outside. "Michael knocked the bowl down." She's crying too. We're all a mess as we wait for the ambulance.

"Maybe we should just take him in ourselves," I suggest, rubbing my hands together, wringing them while looking at the large grove of trees that lead to the main road. Damn it, where are they?

Seeing my panic-stricken face, Santino nods. "Yes, we're going to take him in." Just as he says it, the ambulance comes down the drive.

"What do we have here?"

"He broke Grandma's favorite bowl and was punished for it," Carlotta's three-year-old mouth says. I close my eyes, hoping that they don't take it like she hurt him intentionally.

"Oh, I know. Well, I cut myself two months ago. I leave the cooking to my wife," he tells her.

"That's smart," she informs the medic.

"Okay, let's see how bad this is." They take off the bandage and the cut is pretty rough looking. "Well, it's not as bad as it could be, but he's going to need stitches. Do you want to ride in an ambulance?" he asks Michael.

"With my mommy and daddy?"

He looks at both of us and then notices my large belly. "I don't think it's very comfortable for your mommy, but maybe your dad could ride with you."

"I'll take them in the truck," Martin says.

"Is that okay, tesoro?" Santino asks, staring into my eyes.

"Yes, please just get him to the hospital already so I can stop freaking out."

Before we move away from the porch, they re-bandage his leg with fresh gauze. I go to give him a kiss, and a popping sound is heard, a flow of rushing water follows. "Oh no."

"It looks like Mommy's going to the hospital in the ambulance, but she's going to need the bed. Is that okay?" Michael nods, trying to be a big, brave boy.

Four years later

"Mommy's peeing. Bad Mommy. That's not good even outside. Especially for a girl."

I double over, and Santino's rubbing my back. The time has come for the next little Benedetti.

"We'll follow you guys to the hospital with Carlotta."

"Thank you." They load us into the ambulance. Santino's holding Michael while his leg rests on the edge of the stretcher. I'm lying on it in almost a sitting position. They call out to the hospital and inform them of the situation.

"How far along are you?"

"Thirty-eight weeks," Santino answers as the first contraction hits me.

"It's going to be okay, Mama."

"Thank you, big boy."

Santino

I want to be by Giada's side, but I can't leave Michael alone. Yet, the contractions are coming quick. Thankfully, they give Michael four stitches and then I carry him out to Grandma and Martin. "I have to go to Giada." I kiss my kids' foreheads and run back to the labor and delivery room.

I just make it inside to hold her hand for the most crucial moment. "I'm sorry. I love you so much, but I couldn't leave Michael."

"No, I know. You're a wonderful husband and father-rrr," she cries out the last part as she pushes our son's shoulders out. A loud wail from between her legs echoes in the room and causes my heart to squeeze. I love watching my babies come into this world by my queen.

"Congratulations, Mr. and Mrs. Benedetti. You have a big baby boy with an apparently healthy set of lungs."

They place Gio on Giada's chest, and it never ceases to amaze me how lucky I am. "I have a feeling this one is going to give us trouble."

"He's definitely going to keep us on our toes." They take Gio to clean him off. Smiling and watching them work, I add, "I'd have it no other way." I kiss her lips, wondering if I should tell her that Carlotta told the whole ER that her mama peed on herself and needs a timeout.

"By the way, is Carlotta shouting out to everyone that I peed on myself?"

"How did you know?" The little girl's a chatterbox with no off switch. I love her to pieces. She's what I imagine Giada would have been if she'd been given the proper love a child should have.

"She could never be in the mafia. She has no filter at all."

"Thank God for that."

THE END

Printed in Great Britain
by Amazon